Dred Scott

The Dred Scott Decision

Opinion of Chief Justice Taney

Dred Scott

The Dred Scott Decision
Opinion of Chief Justice Taney

ISBN/EAN: 9783337427689

Printed in Europe, USA, Canada, Australia, Japan

Cover: Foto ©Andreas Hilbeck / pixelio.de

More available books at **www.hansebooks.com**

THE DRED SCOTT DECISION.

OPINION OF CHIEF JUSTICE TANEY,

WITH

AN INTRODUCTION

BY

DR. J. H. VAN EVRIE.

ALSO,

AN APPENDIX,

CONTAINING AN ESSAY ON THE

NATURAL HISTORY OF THE PROGNATHOUS RACE

Of Mankind,

ORIGINALLY WRITTEN FOR THE NEW YORK DAY-BOOK,

BY

DR. S. A. CARTWRIGHT,

OF NEW ORLEANS.

NEW YORK:

VAN EVRIE, HORTON & CO.,

No. 162 NASSAU STREET.

1863.

INTRODUCTION

DR. J. H. VAN EVRIE.

This opinion of Chief Justice Taney and those of his eminent colleagues of the Supreme Court of the Republic, is an epoch in our civil history, which is doubtless destined in all future time to be a land-mark in American civilization.

The facts in the case are all very simple, distinct, common-place, and the conclusions from them plain and unavoidable; nevertheless, this decision, except the Declaration of National Independence in 1776, is the most momentous event that has ever occurred on this continent, and the results destined to flow from it can be second only in importance to those which have followed that memorable event. The Declaration of 1776 announced a truth the most stupendous that ever fell from mere mortal lips—the Dred Scott decision confirms a principle essential to the preservation and success of the former, and which otherwise would needs be but little better than "sounding brass or a tinkling cymbal." Unlike the homogeneous population of Europe, American society is made up of diverse races, each having its own specific wants and necessities, and therefore any social or political organism that is not in accord with these fundamental facts—these unchanging and unchangeable ordinances of the Eternal—must rest on false foundations, and work out evil only to all concerned.

The doctrine of 1776, that all (white) men "are created free and equal," is universally accepted and made the basis of all our institutions, State and National, and the relations of citizenship—the rights of the individual—in short, the *status* of the dominant race, is thus defined and fixed for ever.

But there have been doubts and uncertainties in regard to the negro. Indeed, many (perhaps most) American communities have latterly sought to include him in the ranks of citizenship, and force upon him the *status* of the superior race.

This confusion is now at an end, and the Supreme Court, in the Dred Scott decision, has defined the relations, and fixed the *status* of the subordinate race *forever*— for that decision is in accord with the natural relations of the races, and therefore can never perish. It is based on historical and existing facts, which are indisputable, and it is a necessary, indeed unavoidable inference, from these facts.

A few years after Columbus had discovered and planted a Spanish colony in the island of St. Domingo, there were some negroes (slaves) imported from Spain into the island, and they were found to be so superior to the natives as laborers on the Spanish plantations, that others were soon afterwards imported directly from Africa, and finally into all or nearly all of the Spanish possessions. The British colonies in the northern and temperate latitudes did not need this special class or kind of labor, but as they were in possession of vast territories, and labor of every kind needed for the conquest over these barren and boundless solitudes, they, too, imported

African negroes, and when the British dominion was overthrown, all the colonies had more or less of this negro element in their midst.

All these negroes or their progenitors, all ever brought to America in all the colonies on the continent or in the islands, Spanish, Portuguese, French and English, were in the same subordinate position, and sustained the same (slave) relation to the whites; and such a thing as the introduction of a "free" negro is totally unknown in the history of America.

Was there any other condition of these negroes anterior to the history of this continent? Probably not—at all events, history fails to record any such thing. In the entire past in all lands, whenever and wherever white men and negroes have been in juxtaposition, their relations—the mastery of the former and "slavery" of the latter—have been the same (substantially) as that which exists now at the South, and as they were when modern history first takes cognizance of them.

There were, doubtless, as there are now, modifications in regard to detail, but the great foundation principle, the subordination or "slavery" of this negro element was universal, and for two hundred years and upwards unquestioned in a single instance on this continent, or indeed any other. The various American communities legislated on the subject: they protected the "slave" from the vices or cruelty of the master, while they provided for the welfare of the latter and the general security of this species of property; but all this was in view of the existing fact, the natural relation and fundamental principle of mixed societies, the "slavery" of the negro. They regulated, but of course did not establish or institute this so-called slavery; for like the relations of the sexes, of parents and children, &c., it was inherent, pre-existing, and sprung spontaneously from the necessities of human society. The white man was superior—the negro was inferior—and in juxtaposition, society could only exist, and can only exist, by placing them in natural relation to each other, or by the social subordination, or so-called slavery of the negro.

This universal recognition of "slavery" as the natural relation of the races was the basis of the common law, of course, wherever the common law was itself recognized, and as this was the case in all the British colonies, it followed of necessity that "freedom," "free negroism," or legal equality of negroes, was the creature of the *lex loci* or municipal law. The "common law" is neither more nor less than common sense, and the principles of justice applied to the existing condition, or in conformity with the ordinary and universal usages of the people.

These negroes were different and subordinate beings—they were in a different and subordinate social position, when first known or seen by the colonists—their offspring followed the condition of the parents, and this relation to the whites was universally recognized, and therefore being the common usage or universal custom, it formed the basis of all common law decisions on the subject. Or, in other words, this relation—this social subordination, or so-called "slavery," did universally exist, and therefore in all cases where suits were brought, or the law appealed to, where negroes were in issue, the principles of common sense and justice were applied, in conformity with the universal usage. In some of the eastern colonies, there were doubtless exceptions, and indeed great confusion on this subject; but it is an historical fact that in most of the colonies there was no exception or departure from the common usage until the time or about the time of the great revolutionary movement in 1776, and the radical change of political institutions in the New World. The Spaniards, French, &c., it is supposed, were not "blessed" with the "common law," but this "slavery" was universally recognized as the natural position and real *status* of the negro in all their American possessions, and for two hundred years after their first introduction, no legal decision can be found in all America based on any other assumption.

Indeed, it is true, and a truth which any reflecting mind may readily understand, that were the new entirely isolated from the old world, no other conception of the negro would be possible. Our ideas are the results of our perceptions of external objects. The senses perceive and transmit their impressions to the brain, which compares them and determines their character independent of the will. The negro was brought here a " negro slave," a different and subordinate being, and in a different and subordinate social position, harmonising with his essential nature and the wants and welfare of the superior race; therefore the colonists, of themselves or by themselves, of course could form no other conception of him, or rather of the actual facts thus presented to them.

They might, it is true, conceive of modifications of this condition or regulations of this relation, of greater latitude to the negro, or restraint upon his master; but the modern idea of " freedom," that this different being was the *same* being as themselves, or this *subordinate* creature entitled to equality with themselves, would be a mental impossibility, as palpable as that of water running up hill, or of men standing on their heads instead of their feet. The American recognition of "slavery"— of the facts embodied in the negro being—was therefore universal' throughout America, and among colonists, however separated in opinions, habits, and usages in other respects.

Nor was there the slightest change of opinions or modification of usages until the new ideas of 1776 dawned upon the world, and threatened new and startling changes in the whole frame-work of human society. As long as the colonies retained the system—the outward forms of the old political and social order, and recognized the sovereignty of the mother country, the rulers of England were not disposed to meddle with their domestic concerns, and therefore their relations to the negro element of their population, like every thing else, was left to their own control.

But the establishment of a new system on principles hitherto unrecognized among the statesmen of Europe, and which, if successful, would endanger the social order, as they understood it, impelled the British aristocracy of the day to make every effort possible, moral and material, to embarrass and break down institutions so alarming, and as they doubtless believed, so pregnant with mighty mischiefs to the future of society. So long as the colonists conformed to the general European system, or so long as there was no outward contradiction of American and British society, the relation of the whites to the negro element in their midst was never a subject of doubt or difficulty ; and it is reasonable to conclude that if this contradiction had never happened—if the colonies had never thrown off European dominion, and the relations then existing between the white men of this republic and those of England had continued to this day, then we should never have had the slightest trouble in regard to negroes, and such a social monstrosity as a free negro would probably be unknown among us.

But the new notions which then sprung up in men's minds, and the new forms of political society that followed, and which placed the institutions of America in total and irreconcilable contradiction to those of the mother country, resulted in new combinations, and other and unheard of modes of hostility to the new order.

The idea of equal rights, or of natural equality, is as old as the race itself ; for though there are slight differences in the intellectual as in the (natural) physical powers of individuals, all have the same wants, and therefore the sentiment of Democracy is inherent and everlasting in the very organism of the race. But this idea, or sentiment rather, was never before incorporated into the political institutions of mankind, and when it was made the practical and fundamental principle of the new system, it not only placed the institutions of America in direct hostility to those of Europe, but it convinced the upholders of the latter that this hostility could never cease until one or the other was overthrown.

Fortunately, too, for the friends of monarchy and privilege, materials existed which only needed to be adroitly managed to strike a felon and perhaps deadly blow at the new system, without the risks of war, or even those ordinarily dependent on failure of any kind ; and which, if successful at all, would be wholly so, for it was at the centre, the heart, the very sources of life itself, that the blow would be aimed. One-sixth of our population were negroes—a subordinate social element—which, incorporated and amalgamated with the white citizenship, would so debase and deteriorate the latter, that equality would be undermined, lost and annihilated altogether, and Democracy rendered impracticable and impossible for ever.

Will any one doubt this, or venture to say that we might incorporate the negro element of our population with the white citizenship, and yet preserve our institutions, the purity of our principles, the life of our democratic system ? If there are such, they have only to cast their eyes to the populations south of us to witness the ruin, the degradation, the punishment, misery, and even death that follows all such attempts to incorporate different races into the same system ; and the negro element being still further removed from us, would, were the British or abolition theory reduced to practice, bring upon us only a more rapid and more fearful punishment.

It is not to be supposed that English and European statesmen understood this matter, in what way or manner the ruin and overthrow of the new ideas they so dreaded could be accomplished by means of this negro element of our population, but instinct, if not reason, taught them that it might be decisive and overwhelming.

It is, indeed, probable that in the first instance they merely resorted to that traditional maxim of the British aristocracy, divide and conquer, which has come down from the old Norman nobility, and which has been and is now the leading principle of British policy.

Here was one-sixth of the population shut out from all the chances and enjoyments of political and social intercourse, and which, though they were unable to appeal to it, or to use it as a national instrument for attacking the republic in the ordinary way, *might* be wielded in some mode or form, perhaps equally or even more effective, though that mode or form was indefinite and impalpable to the British mind. But be this as it may, or whatever may have been the reasonings of the enemies of democratic institutions, the motives and the results arrived at admit of no doubt whatever. Their system, if it may be called thus, rested on wrong, on falsehood, on the ignorance, poverty, and degradation of the masses—ours on the principles of eternal truth, on the natural and inalienable right of all (white) men to the same political privileges and legal rights; and the instinctive hostility of opposing systems, the innate and irreconcilable conflict of hostile principles, the necessary warfare of truth and falsehood, of right and wrong, of light and darkness, impelled them, and now impels them, and always will impel them, to make war upon us openly or secretly, in the battle-field, or the still more dangerous field of opinion, until one or the other is overthrown, until Democracy and Democratic institutions are the recognized order of European society, or corrupted by European opinion and enfeebled by monarchical influences, we adopt their dogma of a single race, and in vain and impious efforts to reduce it to practice, collapse into the ruin, degradation, and social destruction of our neighbors, the heterogeneous and amalgamated hordes of Mexico, Central America, &c.

This instinctive hostility, blind as it may have been at first, therefore impelled the enemies of liberty to avail themselves of this negro element for the overthrow of liberty. British and European writers set up the theory or dogma of a single race; that the negro, Indian, &c., of America had the same nature, the same wants, and therefore the same rights as white men; and the British government, under the younger Pitt, followed close upon the heels of these writers to reduce the dogma to practice. They began the warfare by an attack on the African "slave" trade ; and under the lead of Wilberforce, perhaps the sleekest and most adroit hypocrite the world ever saw, they enlisted nearly the entire moral and religious sentiment of England, and with the close connection and almost absolute submission of the same classes among ourselves to British opinion, they obtained at the very beginning the support and sympathy of the religious world in behalf of a cause not merely founded on falsehood, but which, if successful, would work out evils to human kind and to all concerned so stupendous as to be beyond the possibilities of our language to measure or to express them. Wilberforce was a narrow-minded bigot, of the most bigoted school of British Toryism, and in his long parliamentary career, probably never missed a vote when new burthens were to be imposed upon the people, or any chance offered for strengthening the tyranny under which the millions groped their way through a dark and cheerless existence; and the simple fact that such a man was the leader and champion of the cause of "humanity" and "liberty," was itself an unmistakable proof of its falsehood. But here, too, as in the subsequent phases of the mighty imposture, multitudes of good, honest, and well-meaning people labored under a misconception. The African "slave" trade, when isolated or viewed by itself, *seemed*, and perhaps was in many respects, cruel and inhuman, and therefore it was natural that moral and religious people were anxious to put it down and interdict it altogether ; but while this was the professed object of the British government, it was, in fact, a mere incident in the British (negro) policy. That policy is now, if it was not then, perfectly clear and distinct. It was, and it is, to reduce to practice the teachings of British and monarchical writers, to equalize races—to "abolish" the distinctions that separate negroes from white men—in short, to carry out in practice the dogma or doctrine of a single race, and putting down the "slave" trade was only an incident, a single step in the monstrous programme. There were other causes also in operation at the time which compelled the British government to make its anti-"slavery" or free negro efforts in America one of the most prominent features of its general policy. The teachings of Voltaire and the Encyclopediasts had borne their fruits, and the long-suffering and voiceless millions in France had risen with a strength as terrible as it was irresistible, sweeping away kings and nobles, and every form of wrong and oppression almost in a single day; and the spirit thus aroused threatened to spread over all Europe, and to accomplish the same results in every nation. The British aristocracy then became the rallying point for the enemies of the people—the centre of hope, the very sheet anchor of the old oppressions, which for centuries had crushed and brutalized the millions, and this pretended love of liberty in America served to blind and delude the masses in England, and thus to reconcile them to the warfare carried on against liberty in Europe. But the five hundred millions wrung from the sweat and toil and degradation and misery of English laborers, to put down the "slave trade," and give liberty to negroes in America, was expended for crushing out liberty as absolutely, though not so directly, as the three thousand millions expended in Europe. Indeed it was infinitely worse and infinitely more atrocious in the results worked out, for to simply crush out the rights of the people in Europe was kindness and mercy in comparison with the evils dependent on the success of their "free" negro policy in America.

With our mental habits borrowed from Europe, and the almost abject submission to British opinion, it is to be expected that these stupendous efforts to delude us into the adoption of British "anti-slavery" ideas, and the support of their "anti-slavery" policy, would be measurably successful. On a hasty and superficial view, it seemed to be the cause of morality and religion, and therefore the Church, the ministry, the entire religious body among us became infected, more or less, with this moral leprosy—a leprosy a thousand times over more fatal, and, when disclosed in its real character, more hideous than ever cursed Jew or Syrian in the days of old. It pervaded all classes and poisoned all minds, and, strangest of all, it perverted the Judiciary; and though lawyers as a class are usually literal and matter-of-fact in their mental habits, they have been led by this world-wide delusion to utterly ignore fact, and distort reason itself into the grossest folly. An English judge had decided that by the common law all white men were free in England, and therefore discharged a negro from the control of his master, who had brought him to London! This English precedent, like most British precedents, was accepted by our Courts as the rule, unquestioned and unquestionable, and therefore "slavery" became with American jurists, as well as politicians, the creature of the *lex loci*, without name or habitation in the world, except that given it by municipal law; and yet no such law could be found, or can now be found in all America! And this ruling of Chief Justice Mansfield, until quite recently, has been universally admitted. Mr. Clay, Mr. Webster, Colonel Benton—all the great lawyers and eminent legislators, have assumed that "slavery," the social subordination of the negro, the natural relation of the diverse elements that compose our population, was established by municipal law, and therefore could have no existence beyond the sphere of such law!

Such had been the British precedent, and their opinions, already perverted by British and European writers. They never doubted its soundness, though it obviously has no foundation of fact, and therefore involves a palpable absurdity. For many years but little mischief attended the false theories and absurd assumptions prevailing on the subject as far as these States were concerned, though the practical anti-"slavery" policy of England has demoralized and destroyed the countries south of our limits.

But a time has now come when this falsehood and folly can be indulged no longer without carrying with it infinite danger—indeed, the certainty of destruction to the Union itself—in fact, the least of evils, in comparison with the practical success of the British or anti-slavery theory. The negro element has expanded into four millions—every one knows that it must remain here forever—it is rapidly increasing, and the time, therefore, is at hand when the false theories so long imposed on our people must be exploded, and the true *status* of this race fixed beyond question. It therefore was no accident, still less was it by management of any kind, that this Dred Scott case was brought before the Supreme Court for a final decision by the highest legal authority in the Republic or on the continent. The facts in the case, as stated elsewhere, were perfectly simple, and the inference from these facts unavoidable. A master had carried his "slave" (Dred Scott) into the federal Territories, and as there was no local or municipal law *establishing* "slavery" in these Territories, according to the rule laid down by the English chief justice, and so long and disgracefully submitted to by American courts, the "slave" was entitled to freedom! But the Supreme Court, confining itself to the actual, historical and material facts involved, reversed the foreign and monarchical rule. The progenitors of this negro (Dred Scott) were brought here "slaves;" the offspring followed the condition of the parents—there was no local law or municipal regulation altering this condition in the present instance—therefore Dred Scott remained in that condition, a so-called slave.

Could anything be clearer, more logical or truthful, than this decision? Of course, slavery or freedom has nothing to do with the matter. *They* are terms of comparison, having reference to conditions of our own race, and are utter perversions, misapplications, absurdities, when applied to negroes; but as we have no other terms familiar to the common mind, we must, for the present at least, continue to employ them in this connection. The court simply called on the other side to show any law, if it could, altering the *status* of this negro, and as that did not exist, or was not forthcoming, of course it decided that Dred Scott's condition remained the same as his progenitors', and therefore directed him to be returned to his master. But the anti-"slavery zealots insist that the "Missouri Compromise" was such law; that Congress, having enacted a law forbidding the introduction of negro "slaves," that those carried into the Territory became *ipso facto* free men. This is simply absurd, so far as the *status* of the negro is concerned, whatever may be the political question involved. If Congress had power to exclude " slave" owners from the Territories, it no more followed that the " slave" should become a "free man" than that his skin should become white ; but the court also held that as this was a federation of States, Congress had no power to exclude any class of citizens, and therefore that the Missouri compromise was unconstitutional.

At last, then, and in conclusion, we have reached the culminating point of the wildest, the most senseless, the most disgusting, and withal the most dangerous delusion that ever afflicted an intelligent people, or threatened to destroy the peace, order, and safety of human society.

Whatever the course or the legislation of sovereign States, henceforth and forever the *status* of the negro, his relation to the white citizens, and the rights of the latter in respect to "slave" property, are now clearly defined within the Federal jurisdiction. And this decision must be accepted and sustained by the northern masses, or there must be disunion and dismemberment of the Union ; for the States and people having this negro element in their midst, cannot, even if they would, consent to any compromise in this respect, and therefore if the northern people, led astray by the agents and dupes of the enemies of Democracy, refuse to abide by it, there is for the south no alternative but disunion and the establishment of a new confederacy in conformity with the wants and necessities of southern society. It remains, then, for the honest and patriotic citizens of the North who would avoid this calamity of disunion, and save for their offspring the glorious institutions won by the blood and sacrifices of their fathers, to abandon the false mental habits imposed on them by the enemies of these institutions, and, accepting the fixed and immutable truths of the Dred Scott decision, to regard as enemies to the peace of the country, and indeed to the safety of society, all those who, under the pretence of negro liberty, would render liberty for the white man impossible.

SUPREME COURT OF THE UNITED STATES.

DECEMBER TERM, 1856.

DRED SCOTT

versus

JOHN F. A. SANDFORD.

DRED SCOTT, PLAINTIFF IN ERROR, *v.* JOHN F. A. SANDFORD.

I.

1. Upon a writ of error to a Circuit Court of the United States, the transcript of the record of all the proceedings in the case is brought before this court, and is open to its inspection and revision.
2. When a plea to the jurisdiction, in abatement, is overruled by the court upon demurrer, and the defendant pleads in bar, and upon these pleas the final judgment of the court is in his favor— if the plaintiff brings a writ of error, the judgment of the court upon the plea in abatement is before this court, although it was in favor of the plaintiff—and if the court erred in overruling it, the judgment must be reversed, and a mandate issued to the Circuit Court to dismiss the case for want of jurisdiction.
3. In the Circuit Courts of the United States, the record must show that the case is one in which by the Constitution and laws of the United States, the court had jurisdiction—and if this does not appear, and the court gives judgment either for plaintiff or defendant, it is error, and the judgment must be reversed by this court—and the parties cannot by consent waive the objection to the jurisdiction of the Circuit Court.
4. A free negro of the African race, whose ancestors were brought to this country and sold as slaves, is not a " citizen " within the meaning of the Constitution of the United States.
5. When the Constitution was adopted, they were not regarded in any of the States as members of the community which constituted the State, and were not numbered among its " people or citizens." Consequently, the special rights and immunities guarantied to citizens do not apply to them. And not being " citizens " within the meaning of the Constitution, they are not entitled to sue in that character in a court of the United States, and the Circuit Court has not jurisdiction in such a suit.
6. The only two clauses in the Constitution which point to this race, treat them as persons whom it was morally lawful to deal in as articles of property and to hold as slaves.
7. Since the adoption of the Constitution of the United States, no state can by any subsequent law make a foreigner or any other description of persons citizens of the United States, nor entitle them to the rights and privileges secured to citizens by that instrument.
8. A State, by its laws passed since the adoption of the Constitution, may put a foreigner or any other description of persons upon a footing with its own citizens, as to all the rights and privileges enjoyed by them within its dominion, and by its laws. But that will not make him a citizen of the United States, nor entitle him to sue in its courts, nor to any of the privileges and immunities of a citizen in another State.
9. The change in public opinion and feeling in relation to the African race, which has taken place since the adoption of the Constitution, cannot change its construction and meaning, and it must be construed and administered now according to its true meaning and intention when it was formed and adopted.
10. The plaintiff having admitted, by his demurrer to the plea in abatement, that his ancestors were imported from Africa and sold as slaves, he is not a citizen of the State of Missouri according to the Constitution of the United States, and was not entitled to sue in that character in the Circuit Court.
11. This being the case, the judgment of the court below, in favor of the plaintiff on the plea in abatement, was erroneous.

II.

1. But if the plea in abatement is not brought up by this writ of error, the objection to the citizenship of the plaintiff is still apparent on the record, as he himself, in making out his case, states that he is of African descent, was born a slave, and claims that he and his family became entitled to freedom by being taken by their owner to reside in a territory where slavery is prohibited by act of Congress—and that, in addition to this claim, he himself became entitled to freedom by being taken in Rock Island, in the State of Illinois—and being free when he was brought back to Missouri, he was by the laws of that State a citizen.

2. If, therefore, the facts he states do not give him or his family a right to freedom, the plaintiff is still a slave, and not entitled to sue as a "citizen," and the judgment of the Circuit Court was erroneous on that ground also, without any reference to the plea in abatement.

3. The Circuit Court can give no judgment for plaintiff or defendant in a case where it has not jurisdiction, no matter whether there be a plea in abatement or not. And unless it appears upon the face of the record, when brought here by writ of error, that the Circuit Court had jurisdiction, the judgment must be reversed.

The case of Capron v. Van Noorden (2 Cranch, 126) examined, and the principles thereby decided, reaffirmed.

4. When the record, as brought here by writ of error, does not show that the Circuit Court had jurisdiction, this court has jurisdiction to revise and correct the error, like any other error in the court below. It does not and cannot dismiss the case for want of jurisdiction here; for that would leave the erroneous judgment of the court below in full force, and the party injured without remedy. But it must reverse the judgment, and, as in any other case of reversal, send a mandate to the Circuit Court to conform its judgment to the opinion of this court.

5. The difference of the jurisdiction in this court in the cases of writs of error to State courts and to Circuit Courts of the United States, pointed out; and the mistakes made as to the jurisdiction of this court in the latter case, by confounding it with its limited jurisdiction in the former,

6. If the court reverses a judgment upon the ground that it appears by a particular part of the record that the Circuit Court had not jurisdiction, it does not take away the jurisdiction of this court to examine into and correct, by a reversal of the judgment, any other errors, either as to the jurisdiction or any other matter, where it appears from other parts of the record that the Circuit Court had fallen into error. On the contrary, it is the daily and familiar practice of this court to reverse on several grounds, where more than one error appears to have been committed. And the error of a Circuit Court in its jurisdiction stands on the same ground, and is to be treated in the same manner as any other error upon which its judgment is founded.

7. The decision, therefore, that the judgment of the Circuit Court upon the plea in abatement is erroneous, is no reason why the alleged error apparent in the exception should not also be examined, and the judgment reversed on that ground also, if it discloses a want of jurisdiction in the Circuit Court.

It is often the duty of this court, after having decided that a particular decision of the Circuit Court was erroneous, to examine into other alleged errors, and to correct them if they are found to exist. And this has been uniformly done by this court, when the questions are in any degree connected with the controversy, and the silence of the court might create doubts which would lead to further and useless litigation.

III.

1. The facts upon which the plaintiff relies did not give him his freedom, and make him a citizen of Missouri.

2. The clause in the Constitution authorising Congress to make all needful rules and regulations for the government of the territory and other property of the United States, applies only to territory within the chartered limits of some one of the States when they were colonies of Great Britain, and which was surrendered by the British Government to the old Confederation of the States, in the treaty of peace. It does not apply to territory acquired by the present Federal Government, by treaty or conquest, from a foreign nation.

The case of the American and Ocean Insurance Companies v. Canter (1 Peters, 511) referred to and examined, showing that the decision in this case is not in conflict with that opinion, and that the court did not, in the case referred to, decide upon the construction of the clause of the Constitution above mentioned, because the case before them did not make it necessary to decide the question.

3. The United States, under the present Constitution, cannot acquire territory to be held as a colony, to be governed at its will and pleasure. But it may acquire territory which, at the time, has not a population that fits it to become a State, and may govern it as a Territory until it has a population which, in the judgment of Congress, entitles it to be admitted as a State of the Union.

4. During the time it remains a Territory, Congress may legislate over it within the scope of its constitutional powers in relation to citizens of the United States—and may establish a Territorial Government—and the form of this local Government must be regulated by the discretion of Congress, but with powers not exceeding those which Congress itself, by the Constitution, is authorised to exercise over citizens of the United States, in respect to their rights of persons or rights of property.

IV.

1. The territory thus acquired, is acquired by the people of the United States for their common and equal benefit, through their agent and trustee, the Federal Government. Congress can exercise no power over the rights of persons or property of a citizen in the Territory which is prohibited by the Constitution. The Government and the citizen, whenever the Territory is open to settlement, both enter it with their respective rights defined and limited by the Constitution.

2. Congress have no right to prohibit the citizens of any particular State or States from taking with their home there, while it permits citizens of other States to do so. Nor has it a right to give privileges to one class of citizens which it refuses to another. The territory is acquired for their equal and common benefit—and if open to any, it must be open to all upon equal and the same terms.

3. Every citizen has a right to take with him into the Territory any article of property which the Constitution of the United States recognises as property.

4. The Constitution of the United States recognises slaves as property, and pledges the Federal Government to protect it. And Congress cannot exercise any more authority over property of that description than it may constitutionally exercise over property of any other kind.

6. The act of Congress, therefore, prohibiting a citizen of the United States from taking with him his slaves when he removes to the Territory in question to reside, is an exercise of authority over private property which is not warranted by the Constitution—and the removal of the plaintiff, by his owner, to that Territory, gave him no title to freedom.

V

1. The plaintiff himself acquired no title to freedom by being taken, by his owner, to Rock Island, in Illinois, and brought back to Missouri. This court has heretofore decided that the *status* or condition of a person of African descent depended on the laws of the State in which he resided.

2. It has been settled by the decisions of the highest court in Missouri, that by the laws of that State, a slave does not become entitled to his freedom, where the owner takes him to reside in a State where slavery is not permitted, and afterwards brings him back to Missouri.

Conclusion. It follows that it is apparent upon the record that the court below erred in its judgment on the plea in abatement, and also erred in giving judgment for the defendant, when the exception shows that the plaintiff was not a citizen of the United States. And as the Circuit Court had no jurisdiction, either in the case stated in the plea in abatement, or in the one stated in the exception, its judgment in favor of the defendant is erroneous, and must be reversed.

THIS case was brought up, by writ of error, from the Circuit Court of the United States for the district of Missouri.

It was an action of trespass *vi et armis* instituted in the Circuit Court by Scott against Sandford.

Prior to the institution of the present suit, an action was brought by Scott for his freedom in the Circuit Court of St. Louis county, (State court,) where there was a verdict and judgment in his favor. On a writ of error to the Supreme Court of the State, the judgment below was reversed, and the case remanded to the Circuit Court, where it was continued to await the decision of the case now in question.

The declaration of Scott contained three counts: one, that Sandford had assaulted the plaintiff; one, that he had assaulted Harriet Scott, his wife; and one, that he had assaulted Eliza Scott and Lizzie Scott, his children.

Sandford appeared, and filed the following plea:

DRED SCOTT
v.   } Plea to the Jurisdiction of the Court.
JOHN F. A. SANDFORD.

APRIL TERM, 1854.

And the said John F. A. Sandford, in his own proper person, comes and says that this court ought not to have or take further cognizance of the action aforesaid, because he says that said cause of action, and each and every of them, (if any such have accrued to the said Dred Scott,) accrued to the said Dred Scott out of the jurisdiction of this court, and exclusively within the jurisdiction of the courts of the State of Missouri, for that, to wit: the said plaintiff, Dred Scott, is not a citizen of the State of Missouri, as alleged in his declaration, because he is a negro of African descent; his ancestors were of pure African blood, and were brought into this country and sold as negro slaves, and this the said Sandford is ready to verify. Wherefore he prays judgment whether this court can or will take further cognizance of the action aforesaid.

JOHN F. A. SANDFORD.

To this plea there was a demurrer in the usual form, which was argued in April, 1854, when the court gave judgment that the demurrer should be sustained.

In May, 1854, the defendant, in pursuance of an agreement between counsel, and with the leave of the court, pleaded in bar of the action:

1. Not guilty.

2. That the plaintiff was a negro slave, the lawful property of the defendant, and, as such, the defendant gently laid his hands upon him, and thereby had only restrained him, as the defendant had a right to do.

3. That with respect to the wife and daughters of the plaintiff, in the second and third counts of the declaration mentioned, the defendant had, as to them, only acted in the same manner, and in virtue of the same legal right.

In the first of these pleas, the plaintiff joined issue; and to the second and third filed replications alleging that the defendant, of his own wrong and without the cause in his second and third pleas alleged, committed the trespasses, &c.

The counsel then filed the following agreed statement of facts, viz:

In the year 1834, the plaintiff was a negro slave belonging to Dr. Emerson, who was a surgeon in the army of the United States. In that year, 1834, said Dr. Emerson took the plaintiff from the State of Missouri to the military post at Rock Island in the State of Illinois, and held him there as a slave until the month of April or May, 1836. At the time last mentioned, said Dr. Emerson removed the plaintiff from said military post at Rock Island to the military post at Fort Snelling, situate on the west bank of the Mississippi river, in the Territory known as Upper Lousiana, acquired by the United States of France, and situate north of the latitude of thirty-six degrees thirty minutes north, and north of the State of Missouri. Said Dr. Emerson held the plaintiff in slavery at said Fort Snelling, from said last-mentioned date until the year 1838.

In the year 1835, Harriet who is named in the second count of the plaintiff's declaration, was the negro slave of Major Taliaferro, who belonged to the army of the United States. In that year, 1835, said Major Taliaferro took said Harriet to said Fort Snelling, a military post, situated as hereinbefore stated, and kept her there as a slave until the year 1836, and then sold and delivered her as a slave at said Fort Snelling unto the said Dr. Emerson hereinbefore named. Said Dr. Emerson held said Harriet in slavery at said Fort Snelling until the year 1838.

In the year 1836, the plaintiff and said Harriet, at said Fort Snelling, with the consent of said Dr. Emerson, who then claimed to be their master and owner, intermarried, and took each other for husband and wife. Eliza and Lizzie, named in the third count of the plaintiff's declaration, are the fruit of that marriage. Eliza is about fourteen years old, and was born on board the steamboat Gipsey, north of the north line of the State of Missouri, and upon the river Mississippi. Lizzie is about seven years old, and was born in the State of Missouri, at the military post called Jefferson Barracks.

In the year 1838, said Dr. Emerson removed the plaintiff and said Harriet and their said daughter Eliza, from said Fort Snelling to the State of Missouri, where they have ever since resided.

Before the commencement of this suit, said Dr. Emerson sold and conveyed the plaintiff, said Harriet, Eliza, and Lizzie, to the defendant, as slaves, and the defendant has ever since claimed to hold them and each of them as slaves.

At the times mentioned in the plaintiff's declaration, the defendant claiming to be owner as aforesaid, laid his hands upon said plaintiff, Harriet, Eliza and Lizzie, and imprisoned them, doing in this respect, however, no more than what he might lawfully do if they were of right his slaves at such times.

Further proof may be given on the trial for either party.

It is agreed that Dred Scott brought suit for his freedom in the Circuit Court of St. Louis county; that there was a verdict and judgment in his favor; that on a writ of error to the Supreme Court, the judgment below was reversed, and the same remanded to the Circuit Court, where it has been continued to await the decision of this case.

In May 1854, the cause went before a jury, who found the following verdict, viz: "As to the first issue joined in this case, we of the jury find the defendant not guilty; and as to the issue secondly above joined, we of the jury find that before and at the time when, &c., in the first count mentioned, the said Dred Scott was a negro slave, the lawful property of the defendant; and as to the issue thirdly above joined, we, the jury, find that before and at the time when, &c., in the second and third counts mentioned, the said Harriet, wife of said Dred Scott, and Eliza and Lizzie, the daughters of the said Dred Scott, were negro slaves, the lawful property of the defendant."

Whereupon the court gave judgment for the defendant.

After an ineffectual motion for a new trial, the plaintiff filed the following bill of exceptions.

On the trial of this cause by the jury, the plaintiff, to maintain the issues on his part, read to the jury the following agreed statement of facts, (see agreement above.) No further testimony was given to the jury by either party. Thereupon the plaintiff moved the court to give to the jury the following instruction, viz:

"That upon the facts agreed to by the parties, they ought to find for the plaintiff. The court refused to give such instruction to the jury, and the plaintiff, to such refusal, then and there duly excepted."

The court then gave the following instruction to the jury, on motion of the defendant:

"The jury are instructed, that upon the facts in this case, the law is with the defendant." The plaintiff excepted to this instruction.

Upon these exceptions, the case came up to this court.

It was argued at December term, 1855, and ordered to be reargued at the present term.

It was now argued by *Mr. Blair* and *Mr. G. F. Curtis* for the plaintiff in error, and by *Mr. Geyer* and *Mr. Johnson* for the defendant in error.

Mr. Chief Justice TANEY delivered the opinion of the court.

This case has been twice argued. After the argument of the last term, differences of opinion were found to exist among the members of the court; and as the questions in controversy are of the highest importance, and the court was at that time much pressed by the ordinary business of the term, it was deemed advisable to continue the case, and direct a reargument on some of the points, in order that we might have an opportunity of giving to the whole subject a more deliberate consideration. It has accordingly been again argued by counsel, and considered by the court; and I now proceed to deliver its opinion.

There are two leading questions presented by the record :

1. Had the Circuit Court of the United States jurisdiction to hear and determine the case between these parties? And

2. If it had jurisdiction, is the judgment it has given erroneous or not?

The plaintiff in error, who was also the plaintiff in the court below, was, with his wife and children, held as slaves by the defendant, in the state of Missouri ; and he brought this action in the circuit court of the United States for that district, to assert the title of himself and his family to freedom.

The declaration is in the form usually adopted in that State to try questions of this description, and contains the averment necessary to give the court jurisdiction ; that he and the defendant are citizens of different States ; that is, that he is a citizen of Missouri, and the defendant a citizen of New York.

The defendant pleaded in abatement to the jurisdiction of the court, that the plaintiff was not a citizen of the State of Missouri. as alleged in his declaration, being a negro of African descent, whose ancestors were of pure African blood, and who were brought into this country and sold as slaves.

To this plea the plaintiff demurred, and the defendant joined in demurrer. The court overruled the plea, and gave judgment that the defendant should answer over. And he therefore put in sundry pleas in bar, upon which issues were joined ; and at the trial the verdict and judgment were in his favor. Whereupon the plaintiff brought this writ of error.

Before we speak of the pleas in bar, it will be proper to dispose of the questions which have arisen on the plea in abatement.

That plea denies the right of the plaintiff to sue in a court of the United States. for the reasons therein stated.

If the question raised by it is legally before us. and the court should be of opinion that the facts stated in it disqualify the plaintiff from becoming a citizen, in the sense in which that word is used in the Constitution of the United States, then the judgment of the Circuit Court is erroneous and must be reversed.

It is suggested, however, that this plea is not before us ; and that as the judgment in the court below on this plea was in favor of the plaintiff, he does not seek to reverse it, or bring it before the court for revision by his writ of error ; and also that the defendant waived this defence by pleading over, and thereby admitted the jurisdiction of the court.

But in making this objection, we think the peculiar and limited jurisdiction of courts of the United States has not been adverted to. This peculiar and limited jurisdiction has made it necessary, in these courts, to adopt different rules and principles of pleading, so far as jurisdiction is concerned, from those which regulate courts of common law in England, and in the different states of the Union which have adopted the common-law rules.

In these last-mentioned courts, where their character and rank are analogous to that of a Circuit Court of the United States ; in other words, where they are what the law terms courts of general jurisdiction; they are presumed to have jurisdiction, unless the contrary appears. No averment in the pleadings of the plaintiff is necessary, in order to give jurisdiction. If the defendant objects to it, he must plead it specially, and unless the fact on which he relies is found to be true by a jury, or admitted to be true by the plaintiff, the jurisdiction cannot be disputed in an appellate court.

Now, it is not necessary to inquire whether in courts of that description a party who pleads over in bar, when a plea to the jurisdiction has been ruled against him, does or does not waive his plea; nor whether upon a judgment in his favor on the pleas in bar, and a writ of error brought by the plaintiff, the question upon the plea in abatement would be open for revision in the appellate court. Cases that may have been decided in such courts, or rules that may have been laid down by common-law pleaders, can have no influence in the decision in this court. Because, under the Constitution and laws of the United States, the rules which govern the pleadings in its courts, in questions of jurisdiction, stand on different principles and are regulated by different laws.

This difference arises, as we have said, from the peculiar character of the Government of the United States. For although it is sovereign and supreme in its appropriate sphere of action, yet it does not possess all the powers which usually belong to the sovereignty of a nation. Certain specified powers, enumerated in the Constitution, have been conferred upon it; and neither the legislative, executive, nor judicial departments of the Government can lawfully exercise any authority beyond the limits marked out by the Constitution. And in regulating the judicial department, the cases in which the courts of the United States shall have jurisdiction are particularly and specifically enumerated and defined; and they are not authorized to take cognizance of any case which does not come within the description there in specified. Hence, when a plaintiff sues in a court of the United States, it is necessary that he should show, in his pleadings, that the suit he brings is within the jurisdiction of the court, and that he is entitled to sue there. And if he omits to do this, and should, by any oversight of the Circuit Court, obtain a judgment in his favor, the judgment would be reversed in the appellate court for want of jurisdiction in the court below. The jurisdiction would not be presumed, as in the case of a common-law English or State court, unless the contrary appeared. But the record, when it comes before the appellate court, must show, affirmatively, that the inferior court had authority, under the Constitution, to hear and determine the case. And if the plaintiff claims a right to sue in a Circuit Court of the United States, under that provision of the Constitution which gives jurisdiction in controversies between citizens of different States, he must distinctly aver in his pleadings that they are citizens of different States; and he cannot maintain his suit without showing that fact in the pleadings.

This point was decided in the case of Bingham v. Cabot, (in 3 Dall., 382), and ever since adhered to by the court. And in Jackson v. Ashton (8 Pet., 148), it was held that the objection to which it was open could not be waived by the opposite party, because consent of parties could not give jurisdiction.

It is needless to accumulate cases on this subject. Those already referred to, and the cases of Capron v. Van Noorden, (in 2 Cr., 126), and Montalet v. Murray. (4 Cr., 46), are sufficient to show the rule of which we have spoken. The case of Capron v. Van Noorden strikingly illustrates the difference between a common-law court and a court of the United States.

If, however, the fact of citizenship is averred in the declaration, and the defendant does not deny it, and put it in issue by plea in abatement, he cannot offer evidence at the trial to disprove it, and consequently cannot avail himself of the objection in the appellate court, unless the defect should be apparent in some other part of the record. For if there is no plea in abatement, and the want of jurisdiction does not appear in any other part of the transcript brought up by the writ of error, the undisputed averment of citizenship in the declaration must be taken in this court to be true. In this case, the citizenship is averred, but it is denied by the defendant in the manner required by the rules of pleading, and the fact upon which the denial is based is admitted by the demurrer. And, if the plea and demurrer, and judgment of the court below upon it, are before us upon this record, the question to be decided is, whether the facts stated in the plea are sufficient to show that the plaintiff is not entitled to sue as a citizen in a court of the United States.

We think they are before us. The plea in abatement and the judgment of the court upon it, are a part of the judicial proceedings in the Circuit Court, and are there recorded as such; and a writ of error always brings up to the superior court the whole record of the proceedings in the court below. And in the case of the United States v. Smith (11 Wheat., 172,) this court said, that the case being brought up by writ of error, the whole record was under the consideration of this court. And this being the case in the present instance, the plea in abatement is necessarily under consideration; and it becomes, therefore, our duty to decide whether the facts stated in the plea are or are not sufficient to show that the plaintiff is not entitled to sue as a citizen in a court of the United States.

This is certainly a very serious question, and one that now for the first time has been brought for decision before this court. But it is brought here by those who have a right to bring it, and it is our duty to meet it and decide it.

The question is simply this : Can a negro whose ancestors were imported into this country, and sold as slaves, become a member of the political community formed and brought into existence by the Constitution of the United States, and as such become entitled to all the rights and privileges and immunities guarantied to the citizen ? One of which rights is the privilege of suing in a court of the United States in the cases specified in the Constitution.

It will be observed, that the plea applies to that class of persons only whose ancestors were negroes of the African race, and imported into this country, and sold and held as slaves. The only matter in issue before the court, therefore, is, whether the descendants of such slaves, when they shall be emancipated, or who are born of parents who had become free before their birth, are citizens of a State, in the sense in which the word citizen is used in the Constitution of the United States. And this being the only matter in dispute on the pleadings, the court must be understood as speaking in this opinion of that class only, that is, of those persons who are the descendants of Africans who were imported into this country, and sold as slaves.

The situation of this population was altogether unlike that of the Indian race. The latter, it is true, formed no part of the colonial communities, and never amalgamated with them in social connections or in government. But although they were uncivilized, they were yet a free and independent people, associated together in nations or tribes, and governed by their own laws. Many of these political communities were situated in territories to which the white race claimed the ultimate right of dominion. But that claim was acknowledged to be subject to the right of the Indians to occupy it as long as they thought proper, and neither the English nor colonial Governments claimed or exercised any dominion over the tribe or nation by whom it was occupied, nor claimed the right to the possession of the territory, until the tribe or nation consented to cede it. These Indian Governments were regarded and treated as foreign Governments, as much so as if an ocean had separated the red man from the white ; and their freedom has constantly been acknowledged, from the time of the first emigration to the English colonies to the present day, by the different Governments which succeeded each other. Treaties have been negotiated with them, and their alliance sought for in war ; and the people who compose these Indian political communities have always been treated as foreigners not living under our Government. It is true that the course of events has brought the Indian tribes within the limits of the United States under subjection to the white race ; and it has been found necessary, for their sake as well as our own, to regard them as in a state of pupilage, and to legislate to a certain extent over them and the territory they occupy. But they may, without doubt, like the subjects of any other foreign Government, be naturalized by the authority of Congress, and become citizens of a State, and of the United States ; and if an individual should leave his nation or tribe, and take up his abode among the white population, he would be entitled to all the rights and privileges which would belong to an emigrant from any other foreign people.

We proceed to examine the case as presented by the pleadings.

The words "people of the United States" and " citizens " are synonymous terms, and mean the same thing. They both describe the political body who, according to our republican institutions, form the sovereignty, and who hold the power and conduct the Government through their representatives. They are what we familiarly call the " sovereign people," and every citizen is one of this people and a constituent member of this sovereignty. The question before us is, whether the class of persons described in the plea in abatement compose a portion of this people, and are constituent members of this sovereignty ? We think they are not, and that they are not included, and were not intended to be included, under the word "citizens" in the Constitution, and can therefore claim none of the rights and privileges which that instrument provides for and secures to citizens of the United States. On the contrary, they were at that time considered as a subordinate and inferior class of beings, who had been subjugated by the dominant race, and, whether emancipated or not, yet remained subject to their authority, and had no rights or privileges but such as those who held the power and the government might choose to grant them.

It is not the province of the court to decide upon the justice or injustice, the policy or impolicy, of these laws. The decision of that question belonged to the political or law-making power; to those who formed the sovereignty and framed the Constitution. The duty of the court is, to interpret the instrument they have framed, with the best lights we can obtain on the subject, and to administer it as we find it, according to its true intent and meaning when it was adopted.

In discussing this question, we must not confound the rights of citizenship which a State may confer within its own limits, and the rights of citizenship as a member of the Union. It does not by any means follow, because he has all the rights and privileges of a citizen of a State, that he must be a citizen of the United States. He may have all the rights and privileges of the citizen of a State, and yet not be entitled to the rights and privileges of a citizen in any other State. For, previous to the adoption of the Constitution of the United States, every State had the undoubted right to confer on whomsoever it pleased the character of citizen, and to endow him with all its rights. But this character of course was confined to the boundaries of the State, and gave him no rights or privileges in other States beyond those secured to him by the laws of nations and the comity of States. Nor have the several States surrendered the power of conferring these rights and privileges by adopting the Constitution of the United States. Each State may still confer them upon an alien, or any one it thinks proper, or upon any class or description of persons; yet he would not be a citizen in the sense in which that word is used in the Constitution of the United States, nor entitled to sue as such in one of its courts, nor to the privileges and immunities of a citizen in the other States. The rights which he would acquire would be restricted to the State which gave them. The Constitution has conferred on Congress the right to establish an uniform rule of naturalization, and this right is evidently exclusive, and has always been held by this court to be so. Consequently, no State, since the adoption of the Constitution, can by naturalizing an alien invest him with the rights and privileges secured to a citizen of a State under the Federal Government, although, so far as the State alone was concerned, he would undoubtedly be entitled to the rights of a citizen, and clothed with all the rights and immunities which the Constitution and laws of the State attached to that character.

It is very clear, therefore, that no State can, by any act or law of its own, passed since the adoption of the Constitution, introduce a new member into the political community created by the Constitution of the United States. It cannot make him a member of this community by making him a member of its own. And for the same reason it cannot introduce any person or description of persons, who were not intended to be embraced in this new political family, which the Constitution brought into existence, but were intended to be excluded from it.

The question then arises, whether the provisions of the Constitution, in relation to the personal rights and privileges to which the citizen of a State should be entitled, embraced the negro African race, at that time in this country, or who might afterwards be imported, who had then or should afterwards be made free in any State; and to put it in the power of a single State to make him a citizen of the United States, and endue him with the full rights of citizenship in every other State without their consent? Does the Constitution of the United States act upon him whenever he shall be made free under the laws of a State, and raised there to the rank of a citizen, and immediately clothe him with all the privileges of a citizen in every other State, and in its own courts?

The court think the affirmative of these propositions cannot be maintained. And if it cannot, the plaintiff in error could not be a citizen of the State of Missouri, within the meaning of the Constitution of the United States, and, consequently, was not entitled to sue in its courts.

It is true, every person, and every class and description of persons, who were at the time of the adoption of the Constitution recognized as citizens in the several States, became also citizens of this new political body; but none other; it was formed by them, and for them and their posterity, but for no one else. And the personal rights and privileges guarantied to citizens of this new sovereignty were intended to embrace those only who were then members of the several State communities, or who should afterwards by birthright or otherwise become members, according to the provisions of the Constitution and the principles on which it was founded. It was the union of those who were at that time members of distinct and separate political communities into one political family, whose power, for certain specified purposes, was to extend over the whole territory of the United States. And it gave to each citizen rights and privileges outside of his State which he did not before possess, and placed him in every other State upon a perfect equality with its own citizens as to rights of person and rights of property; it made him a citizen of the United States.

It becomes necessary, therefore, to determine who were citizens of the several States when the Constitution was adopted. And in order to do this, we must recur to the governments and institutions of the thirteen colonies, when they separated from Great Britain and formed new sovereignties, and took their places in the family of independent nations. We must enquire who, at that time, were recognized as the people or citizens of a State, whose rights and liberties had been outraged by the English Government; and who declared their independence, and assumed the powers of Government to defend their rights by force of arms.

In the opinion of the court, the legislation and histories of the times, and the language used in the Declaration of Independence, show, that neither the class of persons who had been imported as slaves, nor their descendants, whether they had become free or not, were then acknowledged as a part of the people, nor intended to be included in the general words used in that memorable instrument.

It is difficult at this day to realize the state of public opinion in relation to that unfortunate race, which prevailed in the civilized and enlightened portions of the world at the time of the Declaration of Independence, and when the Constitution of the United States was framed and adopted. But the public history of every European nation displays it in a manner too plain to be mistaken.

They had for more than a century before been regarded as beings of an inferior order, and altogether unfit to associate with the white race, either in social or political relations; and so far inferior, that they had no rights which the white man was bound to respect; and that the negro might justly and lawfully be reduced to slavery for his benefit. He was bought and sold, and treated as an ordinary article of merchandise and traffic, whenever a profit could be made by it. This opinion was at that time fixed and universal in the civilized portion of the white race. It was regarded as an axiom in morals as well as in politics, which no one thought of disputing, or supposed to be open to dispute; and men in every grade and position in society daily and habitually acted upon it in their private pursuits, as well as in matters of public concern, without doubting for a moment the correctness of this opinion.

And in no nation was this opinion nore firmly fixed or more uniformly acted upon than by the English Government and English people. They not only seized them on the coast of Africa, and sold them or held them in slavery for their own use; but they took them as ordinary articles of merchandise to every country where they could make a profit on them, and were far more extensively engaged in this commerce, than any other nation in the world.

The opinion thus entertained and acted upon in England was naturally impressed upon the colonies they founded on this side of the Atlantic. And, accordingly, a negro of the African race was regarded by them as an article of property, and held, and bought and sold as such, in every one of the thirteen colonies which united in the Declaration of Independence, and afterwards formed the Constitution of the United States. The slaves were more or less numerous in the different colonies, as slave labor was found more or less profitable. But no one seems to have doubted the correctness of the prevailing opinion of the time.

The legislation of the different colonies furnishes positive and indisputable proof of this fact.

It would be tedious, in this opinion, to enumerate the various laws they passed upon this subject. It will be sufficient, as a sample of the legislation which then generally prevailed throughout the British colonies, to give the laws of two of them; one being still a large slaveholding State, and the other the first State in which slavery ceased to exist.

The province of Maryland, in 1717, (ch. 13, s. 5,) passed a law declaring "that if any free negro or mulatto intermarry with any white woman, or if any white man shall intermarry with any negro or mulatto woman, such negro or mulatto shall become a slave during life, excepting mulattoes born of white women, who, for such intermarriage, shall only become servants for seven years, to be disposed of as the justices of the county court, where such marriage so happens, shall think fit; to be applied by them towards the support of a public school within the said county. And any white man or white woman who shall intermarry as aforesaid, with any negro or mulatto, such white man or white woman shall become servants during the term of seven years, and shall be disposed of by the justices as afore said, and be applied to the uses aforesaid."

The other colonial law to which we refer was passed by Massachusetts in 1705, (chap. 6.) It is entitled "An act for the better preventing of a spurious and mixed issue," &c.; and it provides, that "if any negro or mulatto shall presume to smite or strike any person of the English or other Christian nation, such negro or mulatto shall be severely whipped, at the discretion of the justices before whom the offender shall be convicted."

And "that none of her Majesty's English or Scottish subjects, nor of any other Christian nation, within this province, shall contract matrimony with any negro or mulatto ; nor shall any person, duly authorised to solemnize marriage, presume to join any such in marriage, on pain of forfeiting the sum of fifty pounds ; one moiety thereof to her Majesty, for and towards the support of the Government within this province, and the other moiety to him or them that shall inform and sue for the same in any of her Majesty's courts of record within the province, by bill, plaint, or information."

We give both of these laws in the words used by the respective legislative bodies, because the language in which they are framed, as well as the provisions contained in them, show, too plainly to be misunderstood, the degraded condition of this unhappy race. They were still in force when the Revolution began, and are a faithful index to the state of feeling towards the class of persons of whom they speak, and of the position they occupied throughout the thirteen colonies, in the eyes and thoughts of the men who framed the Declaration of Independence and established the State Constitutions and Governments. They show that a perpetual and impassable barrier was intended to be erected between the white race and the one which they had reduced to slavery, and governed as subjects with absolute and despotic power, and which they then looked upon as so far below them in the scale of created beings, that intermarriages between white persons and negroes or mulattoes were regarded as unnatural and immoral, and punished as crimes, not only in the parties, but in the person who joined them in marriage. And no distinction in this respect was made between the free negro or mulatto and the slave, but this stigma, of the deepest degradation, was fixed upon the whole race.

We refer to these historical facts for the purpose of showing the fixed opinions concerning that race, upon which the statesmon of that day spoke and acted. It is necessary to do this, in order to determine whether the general terms used in the Constitution of the United States, as to the rights of man and the rights of the people, was intended to include them, or to give to them or their posterity the benefit of any of its provisions.

The language of the Declaration of Independence is equally conclusive :

It begins by declaring " that when in the course of human events it becomes necessary for one people to dissolve the political bands which have connected them with another, and to assume among the powers of the earth the separate and equal station to which the laws of nature and nature's God entitle them, a decent respect for the opinions of mankind requires that they should declare the causes which impel them to the separation."

It then proceeds to say : " We hold these truths to be self-evident : that all men are created equal ; that they are endowed by their Creator with certain unalienable rights ; that among them is life, liberty, and the pursuit of happiness ; that to secure these rights, Governments are instituted, deriving their just powers from the consent of the governed."

The general words above quoted would seem to embrace the whole human family, and if they were used in a similar instrument at this day would be so understood. But it is too clear for dispute, that the enslaved African race were not intended to be included, and formed no part of the people who framed and adopted this declaration ; for if the language, as understood in that day, would embrace them, the conduct of the distinguished men who framed the Declaration of Independence would have been utterly and flagrantly inconsistent with the principles they asserted ; and instead of the sympathy of mankind, to which they so confidently appealed, they would have deserved and received universal rebuke and reprobation.

Yet the men who framed this declaration were great men—high in literary acquirements—high in their sense of honor, and incapable of asserting principles inconsistent with those on which they were acting. They perfectly understood the meaning of the language they used, and how it would be understood by others; and they knew that it would not in any part of the civilized world be supposed to embrace the negro race, which by common consent, had been excluded from civilized Governments and the family of nations, and doomed to slavery. They spoke and acted according to the then established doctrines and principles, and in the ordinary language of the day, and no one misunderstood them. The unhappy black race were separated from the white by indelible marks, and laws long before established, and were never thought of or spoken of except as property, and when the claims of the owner or the profit of the trader were supposed to need protection.

This state of public opinion had undergone no change when the Constitution was adopted, as is equally evident from its provisions and language.

The brief preamble sets forth by whom it was formed, for what purposes, and for whose benefit and protection. It declares that it is formed by the *people* of the United States ; that is to say, by those who were members of the different political communities in the several States ; and its great object is declared to be to secure the blessings of liberty to themselves and their posterity. It speaks in general terms of the *people* of the United States, and of *citizens* of the several States, when it is providing for the exercise of the powers granted or the privileges secured to the citizen. It does not define what description of persons are intended to be included under these terms, or who shall be regarded as a citizen and one of the people. It uses them as terms so well understood, that no further description or definition was necessary.

But there are two clauses in the Constitution which point directly and specifically to the negro race as a separate class of persons, and show clearly that they were not regarded as a portion of the people or citizens of the Government then formed.

One of these clauses reserves to each of the thirteen States the right to import slaves until the year 1808, if it thinks proper. And the importation which it thus sanctions was unquestionably of persons of the race of which we are speaking, as the traffic in slaves in the United States had always been confined to them. And by the other provision the States pledge themselves to each other to maintain the right of property of the master, by delivering up to him any slave who may have escaped from his service, and be found within their respective territories. By the first above-mentioned clause, therefore, the right to purchase and hold this property is directly sanctioned and authorized for twenty years by the people who framed the Constitution. And by the second, they pledge themselves to maintain and uphold the right of the master in the manner specified, as long as the Government they then formed should endure. And these two provisions show, conclusively, that neither the description of persons therein referred to, nor their descendants, were embraced in any of the other provisions of the Constitution ; for certainly these two clauses were not intended to confer on them or their posterity the blessings of liberty, or any of the personal rights so carefully provided for the citizen.

No one of that race had ever migrated to the United States voluntarily ; all of them had been brought here as articles of merchandise. The number that had been emancipated at that time were but few in comparison with those held in slavery ; and they were identified in the public mind with the race to which they belonged, and regarded as a part of the slave population rather than the free. It is obvious that they were not even in the minds of the framers of the Constitution when they were conferring special rights and privileges upon the citizens of a state in every other part of the Union.

Indeed, when we look to the condition of this race in the several States at the time, it is impossible to believe that these rights and privileges were intended to be extended to them.

It is very true, that in that portion of the Union where the labor of the negro race was found to be unsuited to the climate and unprofitable to the master, but few slaves were held at the time of the Declaration of Independence ; and when the Constitution was adopted, it had entirely worn out in one of them, and measures had been taken for its gradual abolition in several others. But this change had not been produced by any change of opinion in relation to this race ; but because it was discovered, from experience, that slave labor was unsuited to the climate and productions of these States : for some of the States, where it had ceased or nearly ceased to exist, were actively engaged in the slave trade, procuring cargoes on the coast of Africa, and transporting them for sale to those parts of the Union where their labor was found to be profitable, and suited to the climate and productions. And this traffic was openly carried on, and fortunes accumulated by it, without reproach from the people of the States where they resided. And it can hardly be supposed that, in the States where it was then countenanced in its worst form—that is, in the seizure and transportation—the people could have regarded those who were emancipated as entitled to equal rights with themselves.

And we may here again refer, in support of this proposition, to the plain and unequivocal language of the laws of the several States, some passed after the Declaration of Independence and before the Constitution was adopted, and some since the Government went into operation.

We need not refer, on this point, particularly to the laws of the present slaveholding States. Their statute books are full of provisions in relation to this class, in the same spirit with the Maryland law which we have before quoted. They have continued to treat them as an inferior class, and to subject them to strict police regulations, drawing a broad line of distinction between the citizen and the slave races, and legislating in relation to them upon the same principle which prevailed at the time of the Declaration of Independence. As relates to these States, it is too plain for argument, that they have never been regarded as a part of the people or citizens of the State, nor supposed to possess any political rights which the dominant race might not withhold or grant at their pleasure. And as long ago as 1822, the Court of Appeals of Kentucky decided that free negroes and mulattoes were not citizens within the meaning of the Constitution of the United States ; and the correctness of this decision is recognized, and the same doctrine affirmed, in 1 Meigs's Tenn. Reports, 331.

And if we turn to the legislation of the States where slavery had worn out, or measures taken for its speedy abolition, we shall find the same opinions and principles equally fixed and equally acted upon.

Thus, Massachusetts, in 1786, passed a law similar to the colonial one of which we have spoken. The law of 1786, like the law of 1705, forbids the marriage of any white person with any negro, Indian, or mulatto, and inflicts a penalty of fifty pounds upon any one who shall join them in marriage; and declares all such marriages absolutely null and void, and degrades thus the unhappy issue of the marriage by fixing upon it the stain of bastardy. And this mark of degradation was renewed and again impressed upon the race, in the careful and deliberate preparation of their revised code published in 1836. This code forbids any person from joining in marriage any white person with any Indian, negro, or mulatto, and subjects the party who shall offend in this respect, to imprisonment, not exceeding six months in the common jail, or to hard labor, and to a fine of not less than fifty nor more than two hundred dollars ; and like the law of 1786, it declares the marriage to be absolutely null and void. It will be seen that the punishment is increased by the code upon the person who shall marry them, by adding imprisonment to a pecuniary penalty.

So, too, in Connecticut. We refer more particularly to the legislation of this State, because it was not only among the first to put an end to slavery within its own territory, but was the first to fix a mark of reprobation upon the African slave trade. The law last mentioned was passed in October, 1788, about nine months after the State had ratified and adopted the present Constitution of the United States; and by that law it prohibited its own citizens, under severe penalties, from engaging in the trade, and declared all policies of insurance on the vessel or cargo made in the State to be null and void. But up to the time of the adoption of the Constitution, there is nothing in the legislation of the State indicating any change of opinion as to the relative rights and position of the white and black races in this country, or indicating that it meant to place the latter, when free, upon a level with its citizens. And certainly nothing which would have led the slaveholding States to suppose that Connecticut designed to claim for them, under the new Constitution, the equal rights and privileges and rank of citizens in every other State.

The first step taken by Connecticut upon this subject was as early as 1774, when it passed an act forbidding the further importation of slaves into the State. But the section containing the prohibition is introduced by the following preamble :

" And whereas the increase of slaves in this State is injurious to the poor, and inconvenient."

This recital would appear to have been carefully introduced, in order to prevent any misunderstanding of the motive which induced the Legislature to pass the law, and places it distinctly upon the interest and convenience of the white population— excluding the inference that it might have been intended in any degree for the benefit of the other.

And in the act of 1784, by which the issue of slaves, born after the time therein mentioned, were to be free at a certain age, the section is again introduced by a preamble assigning a similar motive for the act. It is in these words :

" Whereas sound policy requires that the abolition of slavery should be effected as soon as may be consistent with the rights of individuals, and the public safety and welfare "—showing that the right of property in the master was to be protected, and that the measure was one of policy, and to prevent the injury and inconvenience, to the whites, of a slave population in the State.

And still further pursuing its legislation, we find that in the same statute passed in 1774, which prohibited the further importation of slaves into the State, there is also a provision by which any negro, Indian, or mulatto servant, who was found wandering out of the town or place to which he belonged, without a written pass such as is therein described, was made liable to be seized by any one, and taken before the next authority to be examined and delivered up to his master—who was required to pay the charge which had accrued thereby. And a subsequent section of the same law provides, that if any free negro shall travel without such pass, and shall be stopped, seized, or taken up, he shall pay all charges arising thereby. And this law was in full operation when the Constitution of the United States was adopted, and was not repealed till 1797. So that up to that time free negroes and mulattoes were associated with servants and slaves in the police regulations established by the laws of the State.

And again, in 1833, Connecticut passed another law, which made it penal to set up or establish any school in that State for the instruction of persons of the African race not inhabitants of the State, or to instruct or teach in any such school or institution, or board or harbor for that purpose, any such person, without the previous consent in writing of the civil authority of the town in which such school or institution might be.

And it appears by the case of Crandall v. the State, reported in 10 Conn. Rep., 340, that upon an information filed against Prudence Crandall for a violation of this law, one of the points raised in the defence was, that the law was a violation of the Constitution of the United States ; and that the persons instructed, although of the African race, were citizens of other States, and therefore entitled to the rights and privileges of citizens in the State of Connecticut. But Chief Justice Dagget, before whom the case was tried, held, that persons of that description were not citizens of a State, within the meaning of the word citizen in the Constitution of the United States, and were not therefore entitled to the privileges and immunities of citizens in other States.

The case was carried up to the Supreme Court of Errors of the State, and the question fully argued there. But the case went off upon another point, and no opinion was expressed on this question.

We have made this particular examination into the legislative and judicial action of Connecticut, because, from the early hostility it displayed to the slave trade on the coast of Africa, we may expect to find the laws of that State as lenient and favorable to the subject race as those of any other State in the Union; and if we find that at the time the Constitution was adopted, they were not even there raised to the rank of citizens, but were still held and treated as property, and the laws relating to them passed with reference altogether to the interest and convenience of the white race, we shall hardly find them elevated to a higher rank anywhere else.

A brief notice of the laws of two other States, and we shall pass on to other considerations.

By the laws of New Hampshire, collected and finally passed in 1815, no one was permitted to be enrolled in the militia of the State but free white citizens ; and the same provision is found in a subsequent collection of the laws, made in 1855. Nothing could more strongly mark the entire repudiation of the African race. The alien is excluded, because, being born in a foreign country, he cannot be a member of the community until he is naturalized. But why are the African race, born in the State, not permitted to share in one of the highest duties of the citizen ? The answer is obvious; he is not, by the institutions and laws of the State, numbered among its people. He forms no part of the sovereignty of the State and is not therefore called on to uphold and defend it.

Again, in 1822, Rhode Island, in its revised code, passed a law forbidding persons who were authorized to join persons in marriage, from joining in marriage any white person with any negro, Indian, or mulatto, under the penalty of two hundred dollars, and declaring all such marriages absolutely null and void; and the same law was again re-enacted in its revised code of 1844. So that, down to the last-mentioned period, the strongest mark of inferiority and degradation was fastened upon the African race in that State.

It would be impossible to enumerate and compress in the space usually allotted to an opinion of a court, the various laws, marking the condition of this race, which were passed from time to time after the Revolution, and before and since the adoption of the Constitution of the United States. In addition to those already referred to, it is sufficient to say, that Chancellor Kent, whose accuracy and research no one will question, states in the sixth edition of his Commentaries (published in 1848, 2 vols., 258, note *b*,) that in no part of the country except Maine, did the African race, in point of fact, participate equally with the whites in the exercise of civil and political rights.

The legislation of the States therefore shows, in a manner not to be mistaken, the inferior and subject condition of that race at the time the Constitution was adopted, and long afterwards, throughout the thirteen States by which that instrument was framed; and it is hardly consistent with the respect due to these States, to suppose that they regarded at that time, as fellow-citizens and members of the sovereignty, a class of beings whom they had thus stigmatized; whom, as we are bound, out of respect to the State sovereignties, to assume they had deemed it just and necessary thus to stigmatize, and upon whom they had impressed such deep and enduring marks of inferiority and degradation; or, that when they met in convention to form the Constitution, they looked upon them as a portion of their constituents, or designed to include them in the provisions so carefully inserted for the security and protection of the liberties and rights of their citizens. It cannot be supposed that they intended to secure to them rights, and privileges, and rank, in the new political body throughout the Union, which every one of them denied within the limits of its own dominion. More especially, it cannot be believed that the large slaveholding States regarded them as included in the word citizens, or would have consented to a Constitution which might compel them to receive them in that character from another State. For if they were so received, and entitled to the privileges and immunities of citizens, it would exempt them from the operation of the special laws and from the police regulations which they considered to be necessary for their own safety. It would give to persons of the negro race, who were recognized as citizens in any one State of the Union, the right to enter every other State whenever they pleased, singly or in companies, without pass or passport, and without obstruction, to sojourn there as long as they pleased, to go where they pleased at every hour of the day or night without molestation, unless they committed some violation of law for which a white man would be punished; and it would give them the full liberty of speech in public and in private upon all subjects upon which its own citizens might speak; to hold public meetings upon political affairs, and to keep and carry arms wherever they went. And all of this would be done in the face of the subject race of the same color, both free and slaves, and inevitably producing discontent and insubordination among them, and endangering the peace and safety of the State.

It is impossible, it would seem, to believe that the great men of the slaveholding States, who took so large a share in framing the Constitution of the United States, and exercised so much influence in procuring its adoption, could have been so forgetful or regardless of their own safety and the safety of those who trusted and confided in them.

Besides, this want of foresight and care would have been utterly inconsistent with the caution displayed in providing for the admission of new members into this political family. For, when they gave to the citizens of each State the privileges and immunities of citizens in the several States, they at the same time took from the several States the power of naturalization, and confined that power exclusively to the Federal Government. No State was willing to permit another State to determine who should or should not be admitted as one of its citizens, and entitled to demand equal rights and privileges with their own people, within their own territories. The right of naturalization was therefore, with one accord, surrendered by the States, and confided to the Federal Government. And this power granted to Congress to establish a uniform rule of *naturalization* is, by the well understood meaning of the word, confined to persons born in a foreign country, under a foreign Government. It is not a power to raise to the rank of a citizen any one born in the United States, who, from birth or parentage, by the laws of the country, belongs to an inferior and subordinate class. And when we find the States guarding themselves from the indiscreet or improper admission by other States of emigrants from other countries, by giving the power exclusively to Congress, we cannot fail to see that they could never have left with the States a much more important power—that is, the power of transforming into citizens a numerous class of persons, who in that character would be much more dangerous to the peace and safety of a large portion of the Union, than the few foreigners one of the States might improperly naturalize.

The Constitution upon its adoption obviously took from the States all power by any subsequent legislation to introduce as a citizen into the political family of the United States any one, no matter where he was born, or what might be his character or condition ; and it gave to Congress the power to confer this character upon those only who were born outside of the dominions of the United States. And no law of a State, therefore, passed since the Constitution was adopted, can give any right of citizenship outside of its own territory.

A clause similar to the one in the Constitution, in relation to the rights and immunities of citizens of one State in the other States, was contained in the Articles of Confederation. But there is a difference of language, which is worthy of note. The provision in the Articles of Confederation was "that the *free inhabitants* of each of the States, paupers, vagabonds, and fugitives from justice, excepted, should be entitled to all the privileges and immunities of free citizens in the several States."

It will be observed, that under this Confederation, each State had the right to decide for itself, and in its own tribunals, whom it would acknowledge as a free inhabitant of another State. The term *free inhabitant*, in the generality of its terms, would certainly include one of the African race who had been manumitted. But no example, we think, can be found of his admission to all the privileges of citizenship in any State of the Union after these Articles were formed, and while they continued in force. And, notwithstanding the generality of the words "free inhabitants," it is very clear that, according to their accepted meaning in that day, they did not include the African race, whether free or not: for the fifth section of the ninth article provides that Congress should have the power "to agree upon the number of land forces to be raised, and to make requisitions from each State for its quota in proportion to the number of *white* inhabitants in such State, which requisition should be binding."

Words could hardly have been used which more strongly mark the line of distinction between the citizen and the subject ; the free and the subjugated races. The latter were not even counted when the inhabitants of a State were to be embodied in proportion to its numbers for the general defence. And it cannot for a moment be supposed, that a class of persons thus separated and rejected from those who formed the sovereignty of the States, were yet intended to be included under the words "free inhabitants," in the preceding article, to whom privileges and immunities were so carefully secured in every State.

But although this clause of the Articles of Confederation is the same in principle with that inserted in the Constitution, yet the comprehensive word *inhabitant*, which might be construed to include an emancipated slave, is omitted; and the privilege is confined to *citizens* of the State. And this alteration in words would hardly have been made, unless a different meaning was intended to be conveyed, or a possible doubt removed. The just and fair inference is, that as this privilege was about to be placed under the protection of the General Government, and the words expounded by its tribunals, and all power in relation to it taken from the State and its courts, it was deemed prudent to describe with precision and caution the persons to whom this high privilege was given—and the word *citizen* was on that account substituted for the words *free inhabitant*. The word citizen excluded, and no doubt intended to exclude, foreigners who had not become citizens of some one of the States when the Constitution was adopted; and also every description of persons who were not fully recognised as citizens in the several States. This, upon any fair construction of the instruments to which we have referred, was evidently the object and purpose of this change of words.

To all this mass of proof we have still to add, that Congress has repeatedly legislated upon the same construction of the Constitution that we have given. Three laws, two of which were passed almost immediately after the Government went into operation, will be abundantly sufficient to show this. The two first are particularly worthy of notice, because many of the men who assisted in framing the Constitution, and took an active part in procuring its adoption, were then in the halls of legislation, and certainly understood what they meant when they used the words "people of the United States " and " citizen " in that well-considered instrument.

The first of these acts is the naturalization law, which was passed at the second session of the first Congress, March 26, 1790, and confines the right of becoming citizens "*to aliens being free white persons*"

Now, the Constitution does not limit the power of Congress in this respect to white persons. And they may, if they think proper, authorize the naturalization of any one of any color, who was born under allegiance to another Government. But the language of the law above quoted, shows that citizenship at that time was perfectly understood to be confined to the white race; and that they alone constituted the sovereignty in the government.

Congress might, as we before said, have authorized the naturalization of Indians, because they were aliens and foreigners. But, in their then untutored and savage state, no one would have thought of admitting them as citizens in a civilized community. And, moreover, the atrocities they had but recently committed, when they were the allies of Great Britain in the Revolutionary war, were yet fresh in the recollection of the people of the United States, and they were even then guarding themselves against the threatened renewal of Indian hostilities. No one supposed then that any Indian would ask for, or was capable of enjoying the privileges of an American citizen, and the word white was not used with any particular reference to them.

Neither was it used with any reference to the African race imported into or born in this country; because Congress had no power to naturalize them, and therefore there was no necessity for using particular words to exclude them.

It would seem to have been used merely because it followed out the line of division which the Constitution has drawn between the citizen race, who formed and held the Government, and the African race, which they held in subjection and slavery, and governed at their own pleasure.

Another of the early laws of which we have spoken, is the first militia law, which was passed in 1792, at the first session of the second Congress. The language of this law is equally plain and significant with the one just mentioned. It directs that every "free able-bodied white male citizen" shall be enrolled in the militia. The word *white* is evidently used to exclude the African race, and the word "citizen" to exclude unnaturalized foreigners; the latter forming no part of the sovereignty, owing it no allegiance, and therefore under no obligation to defend it. The African race, however, born in the country, did owe allegiance to the Government, whether they were slaves or free; but it is repudiated, and rejected from the duties and obligations of citizenship in marked language.

The third act to which we have alluded is even still more decisive; it was passed as late as 1813, (2 Stat., 809,) and it provides: "that from and after the termination of the war in which the United States are now engaged with Great Britain, it shall not be lawful to employ, on board of any public or private vessels of the United States, any person or persons except citizens of the United States, *or* persons of color, natives of the United States."

Here the line of distinction is drawn in express words. Persons of color, in the judgment of Congress, were not included in the word citizens, and they are described as another and different class of persons, and authorized to be employed, if born in the United States.

And even as late as 1820, (chap. 104, sec. 8,) in the charter to the city of Washington, the corporation is authorized "to restrain and prohibit the nightly and other disorderly meetings of slaves, free negroes, and mulattoes," thus associating them together in its legislation; and after prescribing the punishment that may be inflicted on the slaves, proceeds in the following words: "And to punish such free negroes and mulattoes by penalties not exceeding twenty dollars for any one offence; and in case of the inability of any such free negro or mulatto to pay any such penalty and cost thereon, to cause him or her to be confined to labor for any time not exceeding six calendar months." And in a subsequent part of the same section, the act authorizes the corporation "to prescribe the terms and conditions upon which free negroes and mulattoes may reside in the city."

This law, like the laws of the States, shows that this class of persons were governed by special legislation directed expressly to them, and always connected with provisions for the government of slaves, and not with those for the government of free white citizens. And after such an uniform course of legislation as we have stated, by the colonies, by the States, and by Congress, running through a period of more than a century, it would seem that to call persons thus marked and stigmatized, "citizens" of the United States, "fellow-citizens," a constituent part of the sovereignty, would be an abuse of terms, and not calculated to exalt the character or an American citizen in the eyes of other nations.

The conduct of the Executive Department of the Government has been in perfect harmony upon this subject with this course of legislation. The question was brought officially before the late William Wirt, when he was the Attorney General of the United States, in 1821, and he decided that the words "citizens of the United States" were used in the acts of Congress in the same sense as in the Constitution; and that free persons of color were not citizens, within the meaning of the Constitution and laws; and this opinion has been confirmed by that of the late Attorney General, Caleb Cushing, in a recent case, and acted upon by the Secretary of State, who refused to grant passports to them as "citizens of the United States."

But it is said that a person may be a citizen, and entitled to that character, although he does not possess all the rights which may belong to other citizens; as, for example, the right to vote, or to hold particular offices; and that yet, when he goes into another State, he is entitled to be recognized there as a citizen, although the State may measure his rights by the rights which it allows to persons of a like character or class resident in the State, and refuse to him the full rights of citizenship.

This argument overlooks the language of the provision in the Constitution of which we are speaking.

Undoubtedly, a person may be a citizen, that is, a member of the community who form the sovereignty, although he exercises no share of the political power, and is incapacitated from holding particular office. Women and minors, who form a part of the political family, cannot vote; and when a property qualification is required to vote or hold a particular office, those who have not the necessary qualification cannot vote or hold the office, yet they are citizens.

So, too, a person may be entitled to vote by the law of the State, who is not a citizen even of the State itself. And in some of the States of the Union foreigners not naturalized are allowed to vote. And the State may give the right to free negroes and mulattoes, but that does not make them citizens of the State, and still less of the United States. And the provision in the Constitution giving privileges and immunities in other States, does not apply to them.

Neither does it apply to a person who, being the citizen of a State, migrates to another State. For then he becomes subject to the laws of the State in which he lives, and he is no longer a citizen of the State from which he removed. And the State in which he resides may then, unquestionably, determine his *status* or condition, and place him among the class of persons who are not recognized as citizens, but belong to an inferior and subject race; and may deny him the privileges and immunities enjoyed by its citizens.   .

But so far as mere rights of persons are concerned, the provision in question is confined to citizens of a State who are temporarily in another State without taking up their residence there. It gives them no political rights in the State, as to voting or holding office, or in any other respect. For a citizen of one State has no right to participate in the government of another. But if he ranks as a citizen in the State to which he belongs, within the meaning of the Constitution of the United States, then, whenever he goes into another State, the Constitution clothes him, as to the rights of person, with all the privileges and immunities which belong to citizens of the State. And if persons of the African race are citizens of a State, and of the United States, they would be entitled to all these privileges and immunities in every State, and the State could not restrict them; for they would hold these privileges and immunities under the paramount authority of the Federal Government, and its courts would be bound to maintain and enforce them, the Constitution and laws of the State to the contrary notwithstanding. And if the States could limit or restrict them, or place the party in an inferior grade, this clause of the Constitution would be unmeaning, and could have no operation; and would give no rights to the citizen when in another State. He would have none but what the State itself chose to allow him. This is evidently not the construction or meaning of the clause in question. It guaranties rights, to the citizen, and the State cannot withhold them. And these rights are of a character and would lead to consequences which make it absolutely certain that the African race were not included under the name of citizens of a State, and were not in the contemplation of the framers of the Constitution when these privileges and immunities were provided for the protection of the citizen in other States.

The case of Legrand v. Darnall (2 Peters, 664) has been referred to for the purpose of showing that this court has decided that the descendant of a slave may sue as a citizen in a court of the United States; but the case itself shows that the question did not arise and could not have arisen in the case.

It appears from the report, that Darnall was born in Maryland, and was the son of a white man by one of his slaves, and his father executed certain instruments to manumit him, and devised to him some landed property in the State. This property Darnall afterwards sold to Legrand, the appellant, who gave his notes for the purchase-money. But becoming afterwards apprehensive that the appellee had not been emancipated according to the laws of Maryland, he refused to pay the notes until he could be better satisfied as to Darnall's right to convey. Darnall, in the mean time, had taken up his residence in Pennsylvania, and brought suit on the notes, and recovered judgment in the Circuit Court for the district of Maryland.

The whole proceeding, as appears by the report, was an amicable one; Legrand being perfectly willing to pay the money, if he could obtain a title, and Darnall not wishing him to pay unless he could make him a good one. In point of fact, the whole proceeding was under the direction of the counsel who argued the case for the appellee, who was the mutual friend of the parties, and confided in by both of them, and whose only object was to have the rights of both parties established by judicial decision in the most speedy and least expensive manner.

Legrand, therefore, raised no objection to the jurisdiction of the court in the suit at law, because he was himself anxious to obtain the judgment of the court upon his title. Consequently, there was nothing in the record before the court to show that Darnall was of African descent, and the usual judgment and award of execution was entered. And Legrand thereupon filed his bill on the equity side of the Circuit Court, stating that Darnall was born a slave, and had not been legally emancipated, and could not therefore take the land devised to him, nor make Legrand a good title; and praying an injunction to restrain Darnall from proceeding to execution on the judgment, which was granted. Darnall answered, averring in his answer that he was a free man, and capable of conveying a good title. Testimony was taken on this point, and at the hearing the Circuit Court was of opinion that Darnall was a free man and his title good, and dissolved the injunction and dismissed the bill; and that decree was affirmed here, upon the appeal of Legrand.

Now, it is difficult to imagine how any question about the citizenship of Darnall, or his right to sue in that character, can be supposed to have arisen or been decided in that case. The fact that he was of African descent was first brought before the court upon the bill in equity. The suit at law had then passed into judgment and award of execution, and the Circuit Court, as a court of law, had no longer any authority over it. It was a valid and legal judgment, which the court that rendered it had not the power to reverse or set aside. And unless it had jurisdiction as a court of equity to restrain him from using its process as a court of law, Darnall, if he thought proper, would have been at liberty to proceed on his judgment, and compel the payment of the money, although the allegations in the bill were true, and he was incapable of making a title. No other court could have enjoined him, for certainly no State equity court could interfere in that way with the judgment of a Circuit Court of the United States.

But the Circuit Court as a court of equity certainly had equity jurisdiction over its own judgment as a court of law, without regard to the character of the parties; and had not only the right, but it was its duty—no matter who were the parties in the judgment—to prevent them from proceeding to enforce it by execution, if the court was satisfied that the money was not justly and equitably due. The ability of Darnall to convey did not depend upon his citizenship, but upon his title to freedom. And if he was free, he could hold and convey property, by the laws of Maryland, although he was not a citizen. But if he was by law still a slave, he could not. It was therefore the duty of the court, sitting as a court of equity in the latter case, to prevent him from using its process, as a court of common law, to compel the payment of the purchase-money, when it was evident that the purchaser must lose the land. But if he was free, and could make a title, it was equally the duty of the court not to suffer Legrand to keep the land, and refuse the payment of the money, upon the ground that Darnall was incapable of suing or being sued as a citizen in a court of the United States. The character or citizenship of the parties had no connection with the question of jurisdiction, and the matter in dispute had no relation to the citizenship of Darnall. Nor is such a question alluded to in the opinion of the Court.

Besides, we are by no means prepared to say that there are not many cases, civil as well as criminal, in which a Circuit Court of the United States may exercise jurisdiction, although one of the African race is a party; that broad question is not before the court. The question with which we are now dealing is, whether a person of the African race can be a citizen of the United States, and become thereby entitled to a special privilege, by virtue of his title to that character, and which, under the Constitution, no one but a citizen can claim. It is manifest that the case of Legrand and Darnall has no bearing on that question, and can have no application to the case now before the court.

This case, however, strikingly illustrates the consequences that would follow the construction of the Constitution which would give the power contended for to a State. It would in effect give it also to an individual. For if the father of young Darnall had manumitted him in his lifetime, and sent him to reside in a State which recognized him as a citizen, he might have visited and sojourned in Maryland when he pleased, and as long as he pleased, as a citizen of the United States; and the State officers and tribunals would be compelled, by the paramount authority of the Constitution, to receive him and treat him as one of its citizens, exempt from the laws and police of the State in relation to a person of that description, and allow him to enjoy all the rights and privileges of citizenship without respect to the laws of Maryland, although such laws were deemed by it absolutely essential to its own safety.

The only two provisions which point to them and include them, treat them as property, and make it the duty of the Government to protect it; no other power, in relation to this race, is to be found in the Constitution; and as it is a Government of special, delegated, powers, no authority beyond these two provisions can be constitutionally exercised. The Government of the United States had no right to interfere for any other purpose but that of protecting the rights of the owner, leaving it altogether with the several States to deal with this race, whether emancipated or not, as each State may think justice, humanity, and the interests and safety of society, require. The States evidently intended to reserve this power exclusively to themselves.

No one, we presume, supposes that any change in public opinion or feeling, in relation to this unfortunate race, in the civilized nations of Europe or in this country, should induce the court to give to the words of the Constitution a more liberal construction in their favor than they were intended to bear when the instrument was framed and adopted. Such an argument would be altogether inadmissible in any tribunal called on to interpret it. If any of its provisions are deemed unjust, there is a mode prescribed in the instrument itself, by which it may be amended; but while it remains unaltered, it must be construed now as it was understood at the time of its adoption. It is not only the same in words, but the same in meaning, and delegates the same powers to the Government, and reserves and secures the same rights and privileges to the citizen; and as long as it continues to exist in its present form, it speaks not only in the same words, but with the same meaning and intent with which it spoke when it came from the hands of its framers, and was voted on and adopted by the people of the United States. Any other rule of construction would abrogate the judicial character of this court, and make it the mere reflex of the popular opinion or passion of the day. This court was not created by the Constitution for such purposes. Higher and graver trusts have been confided to it, and it must not falter in the path of duty.

What the construction was at that time, we think can hardly admit of doubt. We have the language of the Declaration of Independence and of the Articles of Confederation, in addition to the plain words of the Constitution itself; we have the legislation of the different States, before, about the time, and since, the Constitution was adopted; we have the legislation of Congress, from the time of its adoption to a recent period; and we have the constant and uniform action of the Executive Department, all concurring together, and leading to the same result. And if anything in relation to the construction of the Constitution can be regarded as settled, it is that which we now give to the word " citizen " and the word "people."

And upon a full and careful consideration of the subject, the court is of opinion, that, upon the facts stated in the plea in abatement, Dred Scott was not a citizen of Missouri within the meaning of the Constitution of the United States, and not entitled as such to sue in its courts; and, consequently, that the Circuit Court had no jurisdiction of the case, and that the judgment on the plea in abatement is erroneous.

We are aware that doubts are entertained by some of the members of the court, whether the plea in abatement is legally before the court upon this writ of error;

but if that plea is regarded as waived, or out of the case upon any other ground, yet the question as to the jurisdiction of the Circuit Court is presented on the face of the bill of exception itself, taken by the plaintiff at the trial; for he admits that he and his wife were born slaves, but endeavors to make out his title to freedom and citizenship by showing that they were taken by their owner to certain places, hereinafter mentioned, where slavery could not by law exist, and that they thereby became free, and upon their return to Missouri became citizens of that State.

Now, if the removal of which he speaks did not give them their freedom, then by his own admission he is still a slave; and whatever opinions may be entertained in favor of the citizenship of a free person of the African race, no one supposes that a slave is a citizen of the State or of the United States. If, therefore, the acts done by his owner did not make them free persons, he is still a slave, and certainly incapable of suing in the character of a citizen.

The principle of law is too well settled to be disputed, that a court can give no judgment for either party, where it has no jurisdiction; and if, upon the showing of Scott himself, it appeared that he was still a slave, the case ought to have been dismissed, and the judgment against him and in favor of the defendant for costs, is, like that on the plea in abatement, erroneous, and the suit ought to have been dismissed by the Circuit Court for want of jurisdiction in that court.

But, before we proceed to examine this part of the case, it may be proper to notice an objection taken to the judicial authority of this court to decide it; and it has been said, that as this court has decided against the jurisdiction of the Circuit Court on the plea in abatement, it has no right to examine any question presented by the exception; and that anything it may say upon that part of the case will be extra-judicial, and mere obiter dicta.

This is a manifest mistake; there can be no doubt as to the jurisdiction of this court to revise the judgment of a Circuit Court, and to reverse it for any error apparent on the record, whether it be the error of giving judgment in a case over which it had no jurisdiction, or any other material error; and this, too, whether there is a plea in abatement or not.

The objection appears to have arisen from confounding writs of error to a State court, with writs of error to a Circuit Court of the United States. Undoubtedly, upon a writ of error to a State court, unless the record shows a case that gives jurisdiction, the case must be dismissed for want of jurisdiction in *this court*. And if it is dismissed on that ground, we have no right to examine and decide upon any question presented by the bill of exceptions, or any other part of the record. But writs of error to a State court, and to a Circuit Court of the United States, are regulated by different laws, and stand upon entirely different principles. And in a writ of error to a Circuit Court of the United States, the whole record is before this court for examination and decision; and if the sum in controversy is large enough to give jurisdiction, it is not only the right, but it is the judicial duty of the court, to examine the whole case as presented by the record; and if it appears upon its face that any material error or errors have been committed by the court below, it is the duty of this court to reverse the judgment, and remand the case. And certainly an error in passing a judgment upon the merits in favor of either party, in a case which it was not authorized to try, and over which it had no jurisdiction, is as grave an error as a court can commit.

The plea in abatement is not a plea to the jurisdiction of this court, but to the jurisdiction of the Circuit Court. And it appears by the record before us, that the Circuit Court committed an error, in deciding that it had jurisdiction, upon the facts in the case, admitted by the pleadings. It is the duty of the appellate tribunal to correct this error; but that could not be done by dismissing the case for want of jurisdiction here—for that would leave the erroneous judgment in full force, and the injured party without remedy. And the appellate court therefore exercises the power for which alone appellate courts are constituted, by reversing the judgment of the court below for this error. It exercises its proper and appropriate jurisdiction over the judgment and proceedings of the Circuit Court, as they appear upon the record brought up by the writ of error.

The correction of one error in the court below does not deprive the appellate court of the power of examining further into the record, and correcting any other material errors which may have been committed by the inferior court. There is certainly no rule of law—nor any practice—nor any decision of a court—which even questions this power in the appellate tribunal. On the contrary, it is the daily practice of this court, and of all appellate courts where they reverse the judgment of

an inferior court for error, to correct by its opinions whatever errors may appear
on the record material to the case; and they have always held it to be their duty to
do so where the silence of the court might lead to misconstruction or future controversy, and the point has been relied on by either side, and argued before the court.

In the case before us, we have already decided that the Circuit Court erred in
deciding that it had jurisdiction upon the facts admitted by the pleadings. And it
appears that, in the further progress of the case, it acted upon the erroneous principle it had decided on the pleadings, and gave judgment for the defendant, where,
upon the facts admitted in the exception, it had no jurisdiction.

We are at a loss to understand upon what principle of law, applicable to appellate
jurisdiction, it can be supposed that this court has not judicial authority to correct
the last-mentioned error, because they had before corrected the former; or by what
process of reasoning it can be made out, that the error of an inferior court in actually pronouncing judgment for one of the parties, in a case in which it had no jurisdiction, cannot be looked into or corrected by this court, because we have decided
a similar question presented in the pleadings. The last point is distinctly presented
by the facts contained in the plaintiff's own bill of exceptions, which he himself
brings here by this writ of error. It was the point which chiefly occupied the attention of the counsel on both sides in the argument—and the judgment which this court
must render upon both errors is precisely the same. It must, in each of them, exercise jurisdiction over the judgment, and reverse it for the errors committed by the
court below; and issue a mandate to the Circuit Court to conform its judgment to
the opinion pronounced by this court, by dismissing the case for want of jurisdiction
in the Circuit Court. This is the constant and invariable practice of this court,
where it reverses a judgment for want of jurisdiction in the Circuit Court.

It can scarcely be necessary to pursue such a question further. The want of
jurisdiction in the court below may appear on the record without any plea in abatement. This is familiarly the case where a court of chancery has exercised jurisdiction in a case where the plaintiff had a plain and adequate remedy at law, and it so
appears by the transcript when brought here by appeal. So also where it appears
that a court of admiralty has exercised jurisdiction in a case belonging exclusively
to a court of common law. In these cases there is no plea in abatement. And for
the same reason, and upon the same principles, where the defect of jurisdiction is
patent on the record, this court is bound to reverse the judgment, although the defendant has not pleaded in abatement to the jurisdiction of the inferior court.

The cases of Jackson v. Ashton and of Caprou v. Van Noorden, to which we have
referred in a previous part of this opinion, are directly in point. In the last-mentioned case, Capron brought an action against Van Noorden in a Circuit Court of
the United States, without showing, by the usual averments of citizenship, that the
court had jurisdiction. There was no plea in abatement put in, and the parties went
to trial upon the merits. The court gave judgment in favor of the defendant with
costs. The plaintiff thereupon brought his writ of error, and this court reversed the
judgment given in favor of the defendant, and remanded the case with directions to
dismiss it, because it did not appear by the transcript that the Circuit Court had
jurisdiction.

The case before us still more strongly imposes upon this court the duty of examining whether the court below has not committed an error, in taking jurisdiction and
giving a judgment for costs in favor of the defendant; for in Capron v. Van Noorden
the judgment was reversed, because it did *not appear* that the parties were citizens
of different States. They might or might not be. But in this case it *does appear*
that the plaintiff was born a slave; and if the facts upon which he relies have not
made him free, then it appears affirmatively on the record that he is not a citizen,
and consequently his suit against Sandford was not a suit between citizens of different States, and the court had no authority to pass any judgment between the parties. The suit ought, in this view of it, to have been dismissed by the Circuit Court,
and its judgment in favor of Sandford is erroneous, and must be reversed.

It is true that the result either way, by dismissal or by a judgment for the defendant, makes very little, if any, difference in a pecuniary or personal point of view
to either party. But the fact that the result would be very nearly the same to the parties in either form of judgment, would not justify this court in sanctioning an error in
the judgment which is patent on the record, and which, if sanctioned, might be
drawn into precedent, and lead to serious mischief and injustice in some future suit.

We proceed, therefore, to inquire whether the facts relied on by the plaintiff entitled him to his freedom.

The case, as he himself states it, on the record brought here by his writ of error, is this :

The plaintiff was a negro slave, belonging to Dr. Emerson, who was a surgeon in the army of the United States. In the year 1834, he took the plaintiff from the State of Missouri to the military post at Rock Island, in the State of Illinois, and held him there as a slave until the month of April or May, 1836. At the time last mentioned, said Dr. Emerson removed the plaintiff from said military post at Rock Island to the military post at Fort Snelling, situate on the west bank of the Mississippi river, in the territory known as Upper Louisiana, acquired by the United States of France, and situate north of the latitude of thirty-six degrees thirty minutes north, and north of the State of Missouri. Said Dr. Emerson held the plaintiff in slavery at said Fort Snelling, from said last-mentioned date until the year 1838.

In the year 1835, Harriet, who is named in the second count of the plaintiff's declaration, was the negro slave of Major Taliaferro, who belonged to the army of the United States. In that year, 1835, said Major Taliaferro took said Harriet to said Fort Snelling, a military post, situated as hereinbefore stated, and kept her there as a slave until the year 1836, and then sold and delivered her as a slave, at said Fort Snelling, unto the said Dr. Emerson hereinbefore named. Said Dr. Emerson held said Harriet in slavery at said Fort Snelling until the year 1838.

In the year 1836, the plaintiff and Harriet intermarried, at Fort Snelling, with the consent of Dr. Emerson, who then claimed to be their master and owner. Eliza and Lizzie, named in the third count of the plaintiff's declaration, are the fruit of that marriage. Eliza is about fourteen years old, and was born on board the steamboat Gipsey, north of the north line of the State of Missouri, and upon the river Mississippi. Lizzie is about seven years old, and was born in the State of Missouri, at the military post called Jefferson Barracks.

In the year 1838, said Dr. Emerson removed the plaintiff and said Harriet, and their said daughter Eliza, from said Fort Snelling to the State of Missouri, where they have ever since resided.

Before the commencement of this suit, said Dr. Emerson sold and conveyed the plaintiff, and Harriet, Eliza, and Lizzie, to the defendant, as slaves, and the defendant has ever since claimed to hold them, and each of them, as slaves.

In considering this part of the controversy, two questions arise: 1. Was he, together with his family, free in Missouri by reason of the stay in the territory of the United States hereinbefore mentioned? And, 2. If they were not, is Scott himself free by reason of his removal to Rock Island, in the State of Illinois, as stated in the above admissions?

We proceed to examine the first question.

The act of Congress, upon which the plaintiff relies, declares that slavery and involuntary servitude, except as a punishment for crime, shall be forever prohibited in all that part of the territory ceded by France, under the name of Louisiana, which lies north of thirty-six degrees thirty minutes north latitude, and not included within the limits of Missouri. And the difficulty which meets us at the threshold of this part of the inquiry is, whether Congress was authorised to pass this law under any of the powers granted to it by the Constitution ; for if the authority is not given by that instrument, it is the duty of this court to declare it void and inoperative, and incapable of conferring freedom upon any one who is held as a slave under the laws of any one of the States.

The counsel for the plaintiff has laid much stress upon that article in the Constitution which confers on Congress the power " to dispose of and make all needful rules and regulations respecting the territory or other property belonging to the United States ;" but, in the judgment of the court, that provision has no bearing on the present controversy, and the power there given, whatever it may be, is confined, and was intended to be confined, to the territory which at that time belonged to, or was claimed by, the United States, and was within their boundaries as settled by the treaty with Great Britain, and can have no influence upon a territory afterwards acquired from a foreign Government. It was a special provision for a known and particular territory, and to meet a present emergency, and nothing more.

A brief summary of the history of the times, as well as the careful and measured terms in which the article is framed, will show the correctness of this proposition.

It will be remembered that, from the commencement of the Revolutionary war, serious difficulties existed between the States, in relation to the disposition of large and unsettled territories which were included in the chartered limits of some of the States. And some of the other States, and more especially Maryland, which had no unsettled lands, insisted that as the unoccupied lands, if wrested from Great Britain, would owe their preservation to the common purse and the common sword, the money arising from them ought to be applied in just proportion among the several States to pay the expenses of the war, and ought not to be appropriated to the use of the State in whose chartered limits they might happen to lie, to the exclusion of the other States, by whose combined efforts and common expense the territory was defended and preserved against the claim of the British Government.

These difficulties caused much uneasiness during the war, while the issue was in some degree doubtful, and the future boundaries of the United States yet to be defined by treaty, if we achieved our independence.

The majority of the Congress of the Confederation obviously concurred in opinion with the State of Maryland, and desired to obtain from the States which claimed it a cession of this territory, in order that Congress might raise money on this security to carry on the war. This appears by the resolution passed on the 6th of September, 1780, strongly urging the States to cede these lands to the United States, both for the sake of peace and union among themselves, and to maintain the public credit; and this was followed by the resolution of October 10th, 1780, by which Congress pledged itself, that if the lands were ceded, as recommended by the resolution above mentioned, they should be disposed of for the common benefit of the United States, and be settled and formed into distinct republican States, which should become members of the Federal Union, and have the same rights of sovereignty, and freedom, and independence, as other States.

But these difficulties became much more serious after peace took place, and the boundaries of the United States were established. Every State, at that time, felt severely the pressure of its war debt; but in Virginia, and some other States, there were large territories of unsettled lands, the sale of which would enable them to discharge their obligations without much inconvenience; while other States, which had no such resource, saw before them many years of heavy and burdensome taxation; and the latter insisted, for the reasons before stated, that these unsettled lands should be treated as the common property of the States, and the proceeds applied to their common benefit.

The letters from the statesmen of that day will show how much this controversy occupied their thoughts, and the dangers that were apprehended from it. It was the disturbing element of the time, and fears were entertained that it might dissolve the Confederation by which the States were then united.

These fears and dangers were, however, at once removed, when the State of Virginia, in 1784, voluntarily ceded to the United States the immense tract of country lying northwest of the river Ohio, and which was within the acknowledged limits of the State. The only object of the State, in making this cession, was to put an end to the threatening and exciting controversy, and to enable the Congress of that time to dispose of the lands, and appropriate the proceeds as a common fund for the common benefit of the States. It was not ceded because it was inconvenient to the State to hold and govern it, nor from any expectation that it could be better or more conveniently governed by the United States.

The example of Virginia was soon afterwards followed by other States, and, at the time of the adoption of the Constitution, all of the States, similarly situated, had ceded their unappropriated lands, except North Carolina and Georgia. The main object for which these cessions were desired and made, was on account of their money value, and to put an end to a dangerous controversy, as to who was justly entitled to the proceeds when the land should be sold. It is necessary to bring this part of the history of these cessions thus distinctly into view, because it will enable us the better to comprehend the phraseology of the article in the Constitution, so often referred to in the argument.

Undoubtedly the powers of sovereignty and the eminent domain were ceded with the land. This was essential, in order to make it effectual, and to accomplish its objects. But it must be remembered that, at that time, there was no Government of the United States in existence with enumerated and limited powers; what was then called the United States, were thirteen separate, sovereign, independent States, which had entered into a league or confederation for their mutual protection and advantage, and the Congress of the United States was composed of the representatives of these separate sovereignties, meeting together, as equals, to discuss and decide on certain measures which the States, by the Articles of Confederation, had agreed to submit to their decision. But this Confederation had none of the attributes of sovereignty in legislative, executive, or judicial power. It was little more than a congress of ambassadors, authorised to represent separate nations, in matters in which they had a common concern.

It was this congress that accepted the cession from Virginia. They had no power to accept it under the Articles of Confederation. But they had an undoubted right, as independent sovereignties, to accept any cession of territory for their common benefit, which all of them assented to ; and it is equally clear, that as their common property, and having no superior to control them, they had the right to exercise absolute dominion over it, subject only to the restrictions which Virginia had imposed in her act of cession. There was, as we have said, no Government of the United States then in existence with special enumerated and limited powers. The territory belonged to sovereignties, who, subject to the limitations above mentioned, had a right to establish any form of Government they pleased, by compact or treaty among themselves, and to regulate rights of person and rights of property in the territory, as they might deem proper. It was by a Congress, representing the authority of these several and separate sovereignties, and acting under their authority and command (but not from any authority derived from the Articles of Confederation,) that the instrument usually called the ordinance of 1787 was adopted; regulating in much detail the principles and the laws by which this territory should be governed; and among other provisions, slavery is prohibited in it. We do not question the power of the States. by agreement among themselves, to pass this ordinance, nor its obligatory force in the territory, while the confederation or league of the States in their separate sovereign character continued to exist.

This was the state of things when the Constitution of the United States was formed. The territory ceded by Virginia belonged to the several confederated States as common property, and they had united in establishing in it a system of government and jurisprudence, in order to prepare it for admission as States, according to the terms of the cession. They were about to dissolve this federative Union, and to surrender a portion of their independent sovereignty to a new Government, which, for certain purposes, would make the people of the several States one people, and which was to be supreme and controlling within its sphere of action throughout the United States; but this Government was to be carefully limited in its powers, and to exercise no authority beyond those expressly granted by the Constitution, or necessarily to be implied from the language of the instrument, and the objects it was intended to accomplish; and as this league of States would, upon the adoption of the new Government, cease to have any power over the territory, and the ordinance they had agreed upon be incapable of execution and a mere nullity, it was obvious that some provision was necessary to give the new Government sufficient power to enable it to carry into effect the objects for which it was ceded, and the compacts and agreements which the States had made with each other in the exercise of their powers of sovereignty. It was necessary that the lands should be sold to pay the war debt; that a Government and system of jurisprudence should be maintained in it, to protect the citizens of the United States who should migrate to the territory, in their rights of person and of property. It was also necessary that the new Government, about to be adopted, should be authorized to maintain the claim of the United States to the unappropriated lands in North Carolina and Georgia, which had not then been ceded, but the cession of which was confidently anticipated upon some terms that would be arranged between the General Government and these two States. And, moreover, there were many articles of value besides this property in land, such as arms, military stores, munitions, and ships of war, which were the common property of the States, when acting in their independent characters as confederates, which neither the new Government nor any one else would have a right to take possession of, or control, without authority from them; and it was to place these things under the guardianship and protection of the new Government, and to clothe it with the necessary powers, that the clause was inserted in the Constitution which gives Congress the power " to dispose of and make all needful rules and regulations respecting the territory or other property belonging to the United States." It was intended for a specific purpose, to provide for the things we have mentioned. It was to transfer to the new Government the property then held in common by the States, and to give to that Government power to apply it to the objects for which it had been destined by mutual agreement among the States before their league was dissolved. It applied only to the property which the States held in common at that time, and has no reference whatever to any territory or other property which the new sovereignty might afterwards itself acquire.

The language used in the clause, the arrangement and combination of the powers, and the somewhat unusual phraseology it uses, when it speaks of the political power to be exercised in the government of the territory, all indicate the design and meaning of the clause to be such as we have mentioned. It does not speak of *any* territory, nor of *Terri'ories*, but uses language which, according to its legitimate meaning, points to a particular thing. The power is given in relation only to *the* territory of the United States—that is, to a territory then in existence, and then known or claimed as the territory of the United States. It begins its enumeration of powers by that of disposing, in other words, making sale of the lands, or raising money from them, which, as we have already said, was the main object of the cession, and which is accordingly the first thing provided for in the article. It then gives the power which was necessarily associated with the disposition and sale of the lands—that is, the power of making needful rules and regulations respecting the territory. And whatever construction may now be given to these words, every one, we think, must admit that they are not the words usually employed by statesmen in giving supreme power of legislation. They are certainly very unlike the words used in the power granted to legislate over territory which the new Government might afterwards itself obtain by cession from a State, either for its seat of Government, or for forts, magazines, arsenals, dock yards, and other needful buildings.

And the same power of making needful rules respecting the territory is, in precisely the same language, applied to the *other* property belonging to the United States—associating the power over the territory in this respect with the power over movable or personal property—that is, the ships, arms, and munitions of war, which then belonged in common to the State sovereignties. And it will hardly be said, that this power, in relation to the last-mentioned objects, was deemed necessary to be thus specially given to the new Government, in order to authorize it to make needful rules and regulations respecting the ships it might itself build, or arms and munitions of war it might itself manufacture or provide for the public service.

No one, it is believed, would think a moment of deriving the power of Congress to make needful rules and regulations in relation to property of this kind from this clause of the Constitution. Nor can it, upon any fair construction, be applied to any property, but that which the new Government was about to receive from the confederated States. And if this be true as to this property, it must be equally true and limited as to the territory, which is so carefully and precisely coupled with it—and like it referred to as property in the power granted. The concluding words of the clause appear to render this construction irresistible; for, after the provisions we have mentioned, it proceeds to say, " that nothing in the Constitution shall be so construed as to prejudice any claims of the United States, or of any particular State."

Now, as we have before said, all of the States, except North Carolina and Georgia, had made the cession before the Constitution was adopted, according to the resolution of Congress of October 10, 1780. The claims of other States, that the unappropriated lands in these two States should be applied to the common benefit, in like manner, was still insisted on, but refused by the States. And this member of the clause in question evidently applies to them, and can apply to nothing else. It was to exclude the conclusion that either party, by adopting the Constitution, would surrender what they deemed their rights. And when the latter provision relates so obviously to the unappropriated lands not yet ceded by the States, and the first clause makes provision for those then actually ceded, it is impossible, by any just rule of construction, to make the first provision general, and extend to all territories, which the Federal Government might in any way afterwards acquire, when the latter is plainly and unequivocally confined to a particular territory; which was a part of the same controversy, and involved in the same dispute, and depended upon the same principles. The union of the two provisions in the same clause shows that they were kindred subjects; and that the whole clause is local, and relates only to lands, within the limits of the United States, which had been or then were claimed by a State; and that no other territory was in the mind of the framers of the Constitution, or intended to be embraced in it. Upon any other construction it would be impossible to account for the insertion of the last provision in the place where it is found, or to comprehend why, or for what object, it was associated with the previous provision.

This view of the subject is confirmed by the manner in which the present Govern ment of the United States dealt with the subject as soon as it came into existence. It must be borne in mind that the same States that formed the Confederation also formed and adopted the new Government, to which so large a portion of their former sovereign powers were surrendered. It must also be borne in mind that all of these same States which had then ratified the new Constitution were represented in the Congress which passed the first law for the government of this territory; and many of the members of that legislative body had been deputies from the States under the Confederation—had united in adopting the ordinance of 1787, and assisted in forming the new Government under which they were then acting, and whose powers they were then exercising. And it is obvious from the law they passed to carry into effect the principles and provisions of the ordinance, that they regarded it as the act of the States done in the exercise of their legitimate powers at the time. The new Government took the territory as it found it, and in the condition in which it was transferred, and did not attempt to undo anything that had been done. And, among the earliest laws passed under the new Government, is one reviving the ordinance of 1787, which had become inoperative and a nullity upon the adoption of the Constitution. This law introduces no new form or principles for its government, but recites, in the preamble, that it is passed in order that this ordinance may continue to have full effect, and proceeds to make only those rules and regulations which were needful to adapt it to the new Government, into whose hands the power had fallen. It appears, therefore, that this Congress regarded the purposes to which the land in this Territory was to be applied, and the form of government and principles of jurisprudence which were to prevail there, while it remained in the Territorial State, as already determined on by the States when they had full power and right to make the decision; and that the new Government, having received it in this condition, ought to carry substantially into effect the plans and principles which had been previously adopted by the States, and which, no doubt, the States anticipated when they surrendered their power to the new Government. And if we regard this clause of the Constitution as pointing to this Territory, with a Territorial Government already established in it, which had been ceded to the States for the purposes hereinbefore mentioned—every word in it is perfectly appropriate and easily understood, and the provisions it contains are in perfect harmony with the objects for which it was ceded, and with the condition of its government as a Territory at the time. We can, then, easily account for the manner in which the first Congress legislated on the subject—and can also understand why this power over the territory was associated in the same clause with the other property of the United States, and subjected to the like power of making needful rules and regulations. But if the clause is construed in the expanded sense contended for, so as to embrace any territory acquired from a foreign nation by the present Government, and to give it in such territory a despotic and unlimited power over persons and property, such as the confederated States might exercise in their common property, it would be difficult to account for the phraseology used, when compared with other grants of power—and also for its association with the other provisions in the same clause.

The Constitution has always been remarkable for the felicity of its arrangement of different subjects, and the perspicuity and appropriateness of the language it uses. But if this clause is construed to extend to territory acquired by the present Government from a foreign nation, outside of the limits of any charter from the British Government to a colony, it would be difficult to say, why it was deemed necessary to give the Government the power to sell any vacant lands belonging to the sovereignty which might be found within it; and if this was necessary, why the grant of this power should precede the power to legislate over it and establish a Government there; and still more difficult to say, why it was deemed necessary so specially and particularly to grant the power to make needful rules and regulations in relation to any personal or movable property it might acquire there. For the words, *other property*, necessarily, by every known rule of interpretation, must mean property of a different description from territory or land. And the difficulty would perhaps be insurmountable in endeavoring to account for the last member of the sentence, which provides that "nothing in this Constitution shall be so construed as to prejudice any claims of the United States or any particular State," or to say how any particular State could have claims in or to a territory ceded by a foreign Government, or to account for associating this provision with the preceding provisions of the clause, with which it would appear to have no connection.

The words "needful rules and regulations" would seem, also, to have been cautiously used for some definite object. They are not the words usually employed by statesmen, when they mean to give the powers of sovereignty, or to establish a Government, or to authorise its establishment. Thus, in the law to renew and keep alive the ordinance of 1787, and to re-establish the Government, the title of the law is: "An act to provide for the government of the territory northwest of the river Ohio." And in the Constitution, when granting the power to legislate over the territory that may be selected for the seat of Government independently of a State, it does not say Congress shall have power " to make all needful rules and regulations respecting the territory;" but it declares that "Congress shall have power to exercise exclusive legislation in all cases whatsoever over such District (not exceeding ten miles square) as may, by cession of particular States and the acceptance of Congress, become the seat of the Government of the United States.

The words " rules and regulations" are usually employed in the Constitution in speaking of some particular specified power which it means to confer on the Government, and not, as we have seen, when granting general powers of legislation. As, for example, in the particular power to Congress "to make rules for the government and regulation of the land and naval forces, or the particular and specific power to regulate commerce ;" " to establish an uniform *rule* of naturalization;" " to coin money and *regulate* the value thereof." And to construe the words of which we are speaking as a general and unlimited grant of sovereignty over territories which the Government might afterwards acquire, is to use them in a sense and for a purpose for which they were not used in any other part of the instrument. But if confined to a particular Territory, in which a Government and laws had already been established, but which would require some alterations to adapt it to the new Government, the words are peculiarly applicable and appropriate for that purpose.

The necessity of this special provision in relation to property and the rights or property held in common by the confederated States, is illustrated by the first clause of the sixth article. This clause provides that "all debts, contracts, and engagements entered into before the adoption of this Constitution, shall be as valid against the United States under this Government as under the Confederation." This provision, like the one under consideration, was indispensable if the new Constitution was adopted. The new Government was not a mere change in a dynasty, or in a form of government, leaving the nation or sovereignty the same, and clothed with all the rights, and bound by all the obligations of the preceding one. But, when the present United States came into existence under the new Government, it was a new political body, a new nation, then for the first time taking its place in the family of nations. It took nothing by succession from the Confederation. It had no right, as its successor, to any property or rights of property which it had acquired, and was not liable for any of its obligations. It was evidently viewed in this light by the framers of the Constitution. And as the several States would cease to exist in their former confederated character upon the adoption of the Constitution, and could not, in that character, again assemble together, special provisions were indispensable to transfer to the new Government the property and rights which at that time they held in common; and at the same time to authorize it to lay taxes and appropriate money to pay the common debt which they had contracted ; and this power could only be given to it by special provisions in the Constitution. The clause in relation to the territory and other property of the United States provided for the first, and the clause last quoted provides for the other. They have no connection with the general powers and rights of sovereignty delegated to the new Government, and can neither enlarge nor diminish them. They were inserted to meet a present emergency, and not to regulate its powers as a Government.

Indeed, a similar provision was deemed necessary, in relation to treaties made by the Confederation ; and when in the clause next succeeding the one of which we have last spoken, it is declared that treaties shall be the supreme law of the land, care is taken to include, by express words, the treaties made by the confederated States. The language is: " and all treaties made, or which shall be made, under the authority of the United States, shall be the supreme law of the land."

Whether, therefore, we take the particular clause in question, by itself, or in connection with the other provisions of the Constitution, we think it clear, that it applies only to the particular territory of which we have spoken, and cannot, by any just rule of interpretation, be extended to territory which the new Government might afterwards obtain from a foreign nation. Consequently, the power which Congress may have lawfully exercised in this Territory, while it remained under a Territorial Government, and which may have been sanctioned by judicial decision, can furnish

no justification and no argument to support a similar exercise of power over territory afterwards acquired by the Federal Government. We put aside, therefore,
any argument, drawn from precedents, showing the extent of the power which the
General Government exercised over slavery in this Territory, as altogether inap-
plicable to the case before us.

But the case of the American and Ocean Insurance Companies v. Canter (1 Pet.,
511) has been quoted as establishing a different construction of this clause of the
Constitution. There is, however, not the slightest conflict between the opinion now
given and the one referred to; and it is only by taking a single sentence out of the
latter and separating it from the context, that even an appearance of conflict can be
shown. We need not comment on such a mode of expounding an opinion of the
court. Indeed it most commonly misrepresents instead of expounding it. And this
is fully exemplified in the case referred to, where, if one sentence is taken by itself,
the opinion would appear to be in direct conflict with that now given; but the
words which immediately follow that sentence show that the court did not mean to
decide the point, but merely affirmed the power of Congress to establish a Government in the Territory, leaving it an open question, whether that power was derived
from this clause in the Constitution, or was to be necessarily inferred from a power
to acquire territory by cession from a foreign Government. The opinion on this
part of the case is short, and we give the whole of it to show how well the selection
of a single sentence is calculated to mislead.

The passage referred to is in page 542, in which the court, in speaking of the
power of Congress to establish a Territorial Government in Florida until it should
become a State, uses the following language :

" In the mean time Florida continues to be a Territory of the United States, governed by that clause of the Constitution which empowers Congress to make all
needful rules and regulations respecting the territory or other property of the United
States. Perhaps the power of governing a Territory belonging to the United States,
which has not, by becoming a State, acquired the means of self government, may
result, necessarily, from the facts that it is not within the jurisdiction of any particular State, and is within the power and jurisdiction of the United States. The right
to govern may be the inevitable consequence of the right to acquire territory. The right
to govern may be the inevitable consequence of the right to acquire territory.
*Whichever may be the source from which the power is derived, the possession of it is
unquestionable.*"

It is thus clear, from the whole opinion on this point, that the court did not mean
to decide whether the power was derived from the clause in the Constitution, or was
the necessary consequence of the right to acquire. They do decide that the power
in Congress is unquestionable, and in this we entirely concur, and nothing will be
found in this opinion to the contrary. The power stands firmly on the latter alternative put by the court—that is, as "*the inevitable consequence of the right to acquire
territory.*"

And what still more clearly demonstrates that the court did not mean to decide
the question, but leave it open for future consideration, is the fact that the case was
decided in the Circuit Court by Mr. Justice Johnson, and his decision was affirmed
by the Supreme Court. His opinion at the circuit is given in full in a note to the
case, and in that opinion he states, in explicit terms, that the clause of the Constitution applies only to the territory then within the limits of the United States, and not
to Florida, which had been acquired by cession from Spain. This part of his opinion
will be found in the note in page 517 of the report. But he does not dissent from the
opinion of the Supreme Court; thereby showing that, in his judgment, as well as that
of the court, the case before them did not call for a decision on that particular point,
and the court abstained from deciding it. And in a part of its opinion subsequent
to the passage we have quoted, where the court speak of the legislative power of
Congress in Florida, they still speak with the same reserve. And in page 546,
speaking of the power of Congress to authorise the Territorial Legislature to establish courts there, the court say: " They are legislative courts, created in virtue of
the general right of sovereignty which exists in the Government, or in virtue of
that clause which enables Congress to make all needful rules and regulations respecting the territory belonging to the United States."

It has been said that the construction given to this clause is new, and now for the
first time brought forward. The case of which we are speaking, and which has
been so much discussed, shows that the fact is otherwise. It shows that precisely
the same question came before Mr. Justice Johnson, at his circuit, thirty years
ago—was fully considered by him, and the same construction given to the clause

in the Constitution which is now given by this court. And that upon an appeal from his decision the same question was brought before this court, but was not decided because a decision upon it was not required by the case before the court.

There is another sentence in the opinion which has been commented on, which even in a still more striking manner shows how one may mislead or be misled by taking out a single sentence from the opinion of a court, and leaving out of view what precedes and follows. It is in page 546, near the close of the opinion, in which the court say: "In legislating for them," (the territories of the United States,) "Congress exercises the combined powers of the General and of a State Government." And it is said, that as a State may unquestionably prohibit slavery within its territory, this sentence decides in effect that Congress may do the same in a territory of the United States, exercising there the powers of a State, as well as the power of the General Government.

The examination of this passage in the case referred to, would be more appropriate when we come to consider in another part of this opinion what power Congress can constitutionally exercise in a Territory, over the rights of person or rights of property of a citizen. But, as it is in the same case with the passage we have before commented on, we dispose of it now, as it will save the court from the necessity of referring again to the case. And it will be seen upon reading the page in which this sentence is found, that it has no reference whatever to the power of Congress over rights of person or rights of property—but relates altogether to the power of establishing judicial tribunals to administer the laws constitutionally passed, and defining the jurisdiction they may exercise.

The law of Congress establishing a Territorial Government in Florida, provided that the Legislature of the Territory should have legislative powers over " all rightful objects of legislation ; but no law should be valid which was inconsistent with the laws and Constitution of the United States."

Under the power thus conferred, the Legislature of Florida passed an act, erecting a tribunal at Key West to decide cases of salvage. And in the case of which we are speaking, the question arose whether the Territorial Legislature could be authorised by Congress to establish such a tribunal, with such powers; and one of the parties, among other objections, insisted that Congress could not under the Constitution authorise the Legislature of the Territory to establish such a tribunal with such powers, but that it must be established by Congress itself; and that a sale of cargo made under its order, to pay salvors, was void, as made without legal authority, and passed no property to the purchaser.

It is in disposing of this objection that the sentence relied on occurs, and the court begin that part of the opinion by stating with great precision the point which they are about to decide.

They say : " It has been contended that by the Constitution of the United States, the judicial power of the United States extends to all cases of admiralty and maritime jurisdiction; and that the whole of the judicial power must be vested 'in one Supreme Court, and in such inferior courts as Congress shall from time to time ordain and establish.' Hence it has been argued that Congress cannot vest admiralty jurisdiction in courts created by the Territorial Legislature."

And after thus clearly stating the point, before them, and which they were about to decide, they proceed to show that these Territorial tribunals were not constitutional courts, but merely legislative, and that Congress might, therefore, delegate the power to the Territorial Government to establish the court in question ; and they conclude that part of the opinion in the following words: "Although admiralty jurisdiction can be exercised in the States in those courts only which are established in pursuance of the third article of the Constitution, the same limitation does not extend to the Territories. In legislating for them, Congress exercises the combined powers of the General and State Governments."

Thus it will be seen by these quotations from the opinion, that the court, after stating the question it was about to decide in a manner too plain to be misunderstood, proceeded to decide it, and announced, as the opinion of the tribunal, that in organizing the judicial department of the Government in a Territory of the United States, Congress does not act under, and is not restricted by, the third article in the Constitution, and is not bound, in a Territory, to ordain and establish courts in which the judges hold their offices during good behaviour, but may exercise the discretionary power which a State exercises in establishing its judicial department, and regulating the jurisdiction of its courts, and may authorize the Territorial Government to establish, or may itself establish, courts in which the judges hold their offices for a term of years only; and may vest in them judicial power upon subjects confided to the judiciary of the United States. And in doing this, Congress undoubtedly exercises the combined power of the General and a State Government. It exercises the discretionary power of a State Government in authorizing the establishment of a court in which the judges hold their appointments for a term of years only, and not during good behaviour; and it exercises the power of the General Government in investing that court with admiralty jurisdiction, over which the General Government had exclusive jurisdiction in the Territory.

No one, we presume, will question the correctness of that opinion; nor is there anything in conflict with it in the opinion now given. The point decided in the case cited has no relation to the question now before the court. That depended on the construction of the third article of the Constitution, in relation to the judiciary of the United States, and the power which Congress might exercise in a Territory in organizing the judicial department of the Government. The case before us depends upon other and different provisions of the Constitution, altogether separate and apart from the one above mentioned. The question as to what courts Congress may ordain or establish in a Territory to administer laws which the Constitution authorizes it to pass, and what laws it is or is not authorized by the Constitution to pass, are widely different—are regulated by different and separate articles of the Constitution, and stand upon different principles. And we are satisfied that no one who reads attentively the page in Peters's Reports to which we have referred, can suppose that the attention of the court was drawn for a moment to the question now before this court, or that it meant in that case to say that Congress had a right to prohibit a citizen of the United States from taking any property which he lawfully held into a Territory of the United States.

This brings us to examine by what provision of the Constitution the present Federal Government, under its delegated and restricted powers, is authorized to acquire territory outside of the original limits of the United States, and what powers it may exercise therein over the person or property of a citizen of the United States, while it remains a Territory, and until it shall be admitted as one of the States of the Union.

There is certainly no power given by the Constitution to the Federal Government to establish or maintain colonies bordering on the United States or at a distance, to be ruled and governed at its own pleasure; nor to enlarge its territorial limits in any way, except by the admission of new States. That power is plainly given; and if a new State is admitted, it needs no further legislation from Congress, because the Constitution itself defines the relative rights and powers, and duties of the State, and the citizens of the State, and the Federal Government. But no power is given to acquire a Territory to be held and governed permanently in that character.

And indeed the power exercised by Congress to acquire territory and establish a Government there, according to its own unlimited discretion, was viewed with great jealousy by the leading statesmen of the day. And in the Federalist, (No. 38,) written by Mr. Madison, he speaks of the acquisition of the Northwestern Territory by the confederated States, by the cession from Virginia, and the establishment of a Government there, as an exercise of power not warranted by the Articles of Confederation, and dangerous to the liberties of the people. And he urges the adoption of the Constitution as a security and safeguard against such an exercise of power.

We do not mean, however, to question the power of Congress in this respect. The power to expand the territory of the United States by the admission of new States is plainly given; and in the construction of this power by all the departments of the Government, it has been held to authorize the acquisition of territory, not fit for admission at the time, but to be admitted as soon as its population and situation would entitle it to admission. It is acquired to become a State, and not to be held as a colony and governed by Congress with absolute authority; and as the propriety of admitting a new State is committed to the sound discretion of Congress, the power to acquire territory for that purpose, to be held by the United States until it is in a suitable condition to become a State upon an equal footing with the other States, must rest upon the same discretion. It is a question for the political department of the Government, and not the judicial; and whatever the political department of the Government shall recognize as within the limits of the United States, the judicial department is also bound to recognize, and to administer in it the laws of the United States, so far as they apply, and to maintain in the Territory the authority and rights of the Government, and also the personal rights and rights of property of individual citizens, as secured by the Constitution. All we mean to say on this point is, that, as there is no express regulation in the Constitution defining the power which the General Government may exercise over the person or property of a citizen in a Territory thus acquired, the court must necessarily look to the provisions and principles of the Constitution, and its distribution of powers, for the rules and principles by which its decision must be governed.

Taking this rule to guide us, it may be safely assumed that citizens of the United States who migrate to a Territory belonging to the people of the United States, cannot be ruled as mere colonists, dependent upon the will of the General Government, and to be governed by any laws it may think proper to impose. The principle upon which our Governments rest, and upon which alone they continue to exist, is the union of States, sovereign and independent within their own limits in their internal and domestic concerns, and bound together as one people by a General Government, possessing certain enumerated and restricted powers, delegated to it by the people of the several States, and exercising supreme authority within the scope of the powers granted to it, throughout the dominion of the United States. A power, therefore, in the General Government to obtain and hold colonies and dependent territories, over which they might legislate without restriction, would be inconsistent with its own existence in its present form. Whatever it acquires, it acquires for the benefit of the people of the several States who created it. It is their trustee acting for them, and charged with the duty of promoting the interests of the whole people of the whole Union in the exercise of the powers specifically granted.

At the time when the Territory in question was obtained by cession from France, it contained no population fit to be associated together and admitted as a State; and it therefore was absolutely necessary to hold possession of it, as a Territory belonging to the United States, until it was settled and inhabited by a civilized community capable of self-government, and in a condition to be admitted on equal terms with the other States as a member of the Union. But, as we have before said, it was acquired by the General Government, as the representative and trustee of the people of the United States, and it must therefore be held in that character for their common and equal benefit; for it was the people of the several States, acting through their agent and representative, the Federal Government, who in fact acquired the Territory in question, and the Government holds it for their common use until it shall be associated with the other States as a member of the Union.

But until that time arrives, it is undoubtedly necessary that some Government should be established in order to organize society, and to protect the inhabitants in their persons and property; and as the people of the United States could act in this matter only through the Government which represented them, and through which they spoke and acted when the Territory was obtained, it was not only within the scope of its powers, but it was its duty to pass such laws and establish such a Government as would enable those by whose authority they acted to reap the advantages anticipated from its acquisition, and to gather there a population which would enable it to assume the position to which it was destined among the States of the Union. The power to acquire necessarily carries with it the power to preserve and apply to the purposes for which it was acquired. The form of government to be established necessarily rested in the discretion of Congress. It was their duty to establish the one that would be best suited for the protection and security of the citizens of the United States, and other inhabitants who might be authorized to take up their abode there, and that must always depend upon the existing condition of the Territory, as to the number and character of its inhabitants, and their situation in the Territory. In some cases a Government, consisting of persons appointed by the Federal Government, would best subserve the interests of the Territory, when the inhabitants were few and scattered, and new to one another. In other instances, it would be more advisable to commit the powers of self-government to the people who had settled in the Territory, as being the most competent to determine what was best for their own interests. But some form of civil authority would be absolutely necessary to organize and preserve civilized society, and prepare it to become a State; and what is the best form must always depend on the condition of the territory at the time, and the choice of the mode must depend upon the exercise of a discretionary power by Congress, acting within the scope of its constitutional authority, and not infringing upon the rights of person or rights of property of the citizen who might go there to reside, or for any other lawful purpose. It was acquired by the exercise of this discretion, and it must be held and governed in like manner, until it is fitted to be a State.

But the power of Congress over the person or property of a citizen can never be a mere discretionary power under our Constitution and form of Government. The powers of the Government and the rights and privileges of the citizen are regulated and plainly defined by the Constitution itself. And when the Territory becomes a part of the United States, the Federal Government enters into possession in the character impressed upon it by those who created it. It enters upon it with its powers over the citizen strictly defined, and limited by the Constitution, from which it derives its own existence, and by virtue of which alone it continues to exist and act as a Government and sovereignty. It has no power of any kind beyond it; and it cannot, when it enters a Territory of the United States, put off its character, and assume discretionary or despotic powers which the Constitution has denied to it. It cannot create for itself a new character separated from the citizens of the United States, and the duties it owes them under the provisions of the Constitution. The Territory being a part of the United States, the Government and the citizen both enter it under the authority of the Constitution, with their respective rights defined and marked out; and the Federal Government can exercise no power over his person or property, beyond what that instrument confers, nor lawfully deny any right which it has reserved.

A reference to a few of the provisions of the Constitution will illustrate this proposition.

For example, no one, we presume, will contend that Congress can make any law in a Territory respecting the establishment of religion, or the free exercise thereof, or abridging the freedom of speech or of the press, or the right of the people of the Territory peaceably to assemble, and to petition the Government for the redress of grievances.

Nor can Congress deny to the people the right to keep and bear arms, nor the right to trial by jury, nor compel any one to be a witness against himself in a criminal proceeding.

These powers, and others, in relation to rights of person, which it is not necessary here to enumerate, are, in express and positive terms, denied to the General Government; and the rights of private property have been guarded with equal care. Thus the rights of property are united with the rights of person, and placed on the same ground by the fifth amendment to the Constitution, which provides that no person shall be deprived of life, liberty, and property, without due process of law. And an act of Congress which deprives a citizen of the United States of his liberty or property, merely because he came himself or brought his property into a particular Territory of the United States, and who had committed no offence against the laws, could hardly be dignified with the name of due process of law.

So, too, it will hardly be contended that Congress could by law quarter a soldier in a house in a Territory without the consent of the owner, in time of peace; nor in time of war, but in a manner prescribed by law. Nor could they by law forfeit the property of a citizen in a Territory who was convicted of treason, for a longer period than the life of the person convicted; nor take private property for public use without just compensation.

The powers over person and property of which we speak are not only not granted to Congress, but are in express terms denied, and they are forbidden to exercise them. And this prohibition is not confined to the States, but the words are general, and extend to the whole territory over which the Constitution gives it power to legislate, including those portions of it remaining under Territorial Government, as well as that covered by States. It is a total absence of power everywhere within the dominion of the United States, and places the citizens of a Territory, so far as these rights are concerned, on the same footing with citizens of the States, and guards them as firmly and plainly against any inroads which the General Government might attempt, under the plea of implied or incidental powers. And if Congress itself cannot do this—if it is beyond the powers conferred on the Federal Government—it will be admitted, we presume, that it could not authorise a Territorial Government to exercise them. It could confer no power on any local Government, established by its authority, to violate the provisions of the Constitution.

It seems, however, to be supposed, that there is a difference between property in a slave and other property, and that different rules may be applied to it in expounding the Constitution of the United States. And the laws and usages of nations, and the writings of eminent jurists upon the relation of master and slave and their mutual rights and duties, and the powers which Governments may exercise over it, have been dwelt upon in the argument.

But in considering the question before us, it must be borne in mind that there is no law of nations standing between the people of the United States and their Government, and interfering with their relation to each other. The powers of the Government, and the rights of the citizen under it, are positive and practical regulations plainly written down. The people of the United States have delegated to it certain enumerated powers, and forbidden it to exercise others. It has no power over the person or property of a citizen but what the citizens of the United States have granted. And no laws or usages of other nations, or reasoning of statesmen or jurists upon the relations of master and slave, can enlarge the powers of the Government, or take from the citizens the rights they have reserved. And if the Constitution recognizes the right of property of the master in a slave, and makes no distinction between that description of property and other property owned by a citizen, no tribunal, acting under the authority of the United States, whether it be legislative, executive, or judicial, has a right to draw such a distinction, or deny to it the benefit of the provisions and guarantees which have been provided for the protection of private property against the encroachments of the Government.

Now, as we have already said in an earlier part of this opinion, upon a different point, the right of property in a slave is distinctly and expressly affirmed in the Constitution. The right to traffic in it, like an ordinary article of merchandise and property, was guarantied to the citizens of the United States, in every State that might desire it, for twenty years. And the Government in express terms is pledged to protect it in all future time, if the slave escapes from his owner. This is done in plain words—too plain to be misunderstood. And no word can be found in the Constitution which gives Congress a greater power over slave property, or which entitles property of that kind to less protection than property of any other description. The only power conferred is the power coupled with the duty of guarding and protecting the owner in his rights.

Upon these considerations, it is the opinion of the court that the act of Congress which prohibited a citizen from holding and owning property of this kind in the territory of the United States north of the line therein mentioned, is not warranted by the Constitution, and is therefore void; and that neither Dred Scott himself, nor any of his family, were made free by being carried into this territory; even if they had been carried there by the owner, with the intention of becoming a permanent resident.

We have so far examined the case, as it stands under the Constitution of the United States, and the powers thereby delegated to the Federal Government.

But there is another point in the case which depends on State power and State law. And it is contended, on the part of the plaintiff, that he is made free by being taken to Rock Island, in the State of Illinois, independently of his residence in the territory of the United States; and being so made free, he was not again reduced to a state of slavery by being brought back to Missouri.

Our notice of this part of the case will be very brief; for the principle on which it depends was decided in this court, upon much consideration, in the case of Strader et al. v. Graham, reported in 10th Howard, 82. In that case, the slaves had been taken from Kentucky to Ohio, with the consent of the owner, and afterwards brought back to Kentucky. And this court held that their status or condition, as free or slave, depended upon the laws of Kentucky, when they were brought back into that State, and not of Ohio; and that this court had no jurisdiction to revise the judgment of a State court upon its own laws. This was the point directly before the court, and the decision that this court had not jurisdiction turned upon it, as will be seen by the report of the case.

So in this case. As Scott was a slave when taken into the State of Illinois by his owner, and was there held as such, and brought back in that character, his status, as free or slave, depended on the laws of Missouri, and not of Illinois.

It has, however, been urged in the argument, that by the laws of Missouri he was free on his return, and that this case, therefore, cannot be governed by the case of Strader et al. v. Graham, where it appeared, by the laws of Kentucky, that the plaintiffs continued to be slaves on their return from Ohio. But whatever doubts or opinions may, at one time, have been entertained upon this subject, we are satisfied, upon a careful examination of all the cases decided in the State courts of

Missouri referred to, that it is now firmly settled by the decisions of the highest court in the State, that Scott and his family upon their return were not free. but were, by the laws of Missouri, the property of the defendant; and that the Circuit Court of the United States had no jurisdiction, when, by the laws of the State, the plaintiff was a slave, and not a citizen.

Moreover, the plaintiff, it appears, brought a similar action against the defendant in the State Court of Missouri, claiming the freedom of himself and his family upon the same grounds and the same evidence upon which he relies in the case before the court. The case was carried before the Supreme Court of the State; was fully argued there; and that court decided that neither the plaintiff nor his family were entitled to freedom, and were still the slaves of the defendant; and reversed the judgment of the inferior State court, which had given a different decision. If the plaintiff supposed that this judgment of the Supreme Court of the State was erroneous, and that this court had jurisdiction to revise and reverse it, the only mode by which he could legally bring it before this court was by writ of error directed to the Supreme Court of the State, requiring it to transmit the record to this court. If this had been done, it is too plain for argument that the writ must have been dismissed for want of jurisdiction in this court. The case of Strader and others *v.* Graham is directly in point; and, indeed, independent of any decision, the language of the 25th section of the act of 1789 is too clear and precise to admit of controversy.

But the plaintiff did not pursue the mode prescribed by law for bringing the judgment of a State court before this court for revision, but suffered the case to be remanded to the inferior State court, where it is still continued, and is, by agreement of parties, to await the judgment of this court on the point. All of this appears on the record before us, and by the printed report of the case.

And while the case is yet open and pending in the inferior State court, the plaintiff goes into the Circuit Court of the United States, upon the same case and the same evidence, and against the same party, and proceeds to judgment, and then brings here the same case from the Circuit Court, which the law would not have permitted him to bring directly from the State court. And if this court takes jurisdiction in this form, the result, so far as the rights of the respective parties are concerned, is in every respect substantially the same as if it had in open violation of law entertained jurisdiction over the judgment of the State court upon a writ of error, and revised and reversed its judgment upon the ground that its opinion upon the question of law was erroneous. It would ill become this court to sanction such an attempt to evade the law, or to exercise an appellate power in this circuitous way, which it is forbidden to exercise in the direct and regular and invariable forms of judicial proceedings.

Upon the whole, therefore, it is the judgment of this court, that it appears by the record before us that the plaintiff in error is not a citizen of Missouri, in the sense in which that word is used in the Constitution; and that the Circuit Court of the United States, for that reason, had no jurisdiction in the case, and could give no judgment in it. Its judgment for the defendant must, consequently, be reversed, and a mandate issued, directing the suit to be dismissed for want of jurisdiction.

APPENDIX.

[From the New York Day-Book, Nov. 10, 1857.]

NATURAL HISTORY OF THE PROGNATHOUS SPECIES OF MANKIND.

BY DR. SAMUEL A. CARTWRIGHT, OF NEW ORLEANS.

It is not intended by the use of the term Prognathous to call in question the black man's humanity or the unity of the human races as a *genus*, but to prove that the species of the genus homo are not a unity, but a plurality, each essentially different from the others—one of them being so unlike the other two—the oval-headed Caucasian and the pyramidal-headed Mongolian—as to be actually prognathous, like the brute creation; not that the negro is a brute, or half man and half brute, but a genuine human being, anatomically constructed, about the head and face, more like the monkey tribes and the lower order of animals than any other species of the genus man. Prognathous is a technical term derived from *pro*, before, and *gnathos*, the jaws, indicating that the muzzle or mouth is anterior to the brain. The lower animals, according to Cuvier, are distinguished from the European and Mongol man by the mouth and face projecting further forward in the profile than the brain. He expresses the rule thus: *face anterior, cranium posterior*. The typical negroes of adult age, when tried by this rule, are proved to belong to a different species from the man of Europe or Asia, because the head and face are anatomically constructed more after the fashion of the simiadiæ and the brute creation than the Caucasian and Mongolian species of mankind, their mouth and jaws projecting beyond the forehead containing the anterior lobes of the brain. Moreover, their faces are proportionally larger than their crania, instead of smaller, as in the other two species of the genus man. Young monkeys and young negroes, however, are not prognathous like their parents, but become so as they grow older. The head of the infant ourang outang is like that of a well formed Caucasian child in the projection and height of the forehead and the convexity of the vertex. The brain appears to be larger than it really is, because the face, at birth, has not attained its proportional size. The face of the Caucasian infant is a little under its proportional size when compared with the cranium. In the infant negro and ourang outang it is greatly so. Although so much smaller in infancy than the cranium, the face of the young monkey ultimately outgrows the cranium; so, also, does the face of the young negro, whereas in the Caucasian, the face always continues to be smaller than the cranium. The superfices of the face at puberty exceeds that of the hairy scalp both in the negro and the monkey, while it is always less in the white man. Young monkeys and young negroes are superior to white children of the same age in memory and other intellectual faculties. The white infant comes into the world with its brain inclosed by fifteen disunited bony plates—the occipital bone being divided into four parts, the sphenoid into three, the frontal into two, each of the two temporals into two, which, with the two parietals, make fifteen plates in all—the vomer and ethmoid not being ossified at birth. The bones of the head are not only disunited, but are more or less overlapped at birth, in consequence of the largeness of the Caucasian child's head and the smallness of its mother's pelvis, giving the head an elongated form, and an irregular, knotty feel to the touch. The negro infant, however, is born with a small, hard, smooth, round head like a gourd. Instead of the frontal and temporal bones being divided into six plates, as in the white child, they form but one bone in the negro infant. The head is not only smaller than that of the white child, but the pelvis of the negress is wider than that of the white woman—its greater obliquity also favors parturition and prevents miscarriage.

Negro children and white children are alike at birth in one remarkable particular—they are both born *white*, and so much alike, as far as color is concerned, as scarcely to be distinguished from each other. In a very short time, however, the skin of the negro infant begins to darken and continues to grow darker until it becomes of a shining black color, provided the child be healthy. The skin will become black whether exposed to the air and light or not. The blackness is not of as deep a shade during the first years of life, as afterwards. The black color is not so deep in the female as in the male, nor in the feeble, sickly negro as in the robust and healthy. Blackness is a characteristic of the prognathous species of the genus homo, but all the varieties of all the prognathous species are not equally black. Nor are the individuals of the same family or variety equally so. The lighter shades of color, when not derived from admixture with Mongolian or Caucasian blood, indicate degeneration in the prognathous species. The Hottentots, Bushmen and aborigines of Australia are inferior in mind and body to the typical African of Guinea and the Niger.

The typical negroes themselves are more or less superior or inferior to one another precisely as they approximate to or recede from the typical standard in color and form, due allowance being made for age and sex. The standard is an oily, shining black, and as far as the conformation of the head and face is concerned and the relative proportion of nervous matter outside of the cranium to the quantity of cerebral matter within it, is found between the simiadiæ and the Caucasian. Thus, in the typical negro, a perpendicular line, let fall from the forehead, cuts off a large portion of the face, throwing the mouth, the thick lips, and the projecting teeth anterior to the cranium, but not the entire face, as in the lower animals and monkey tribes. When all, or a greater part of the face is thrown anterior to the line, the negro approximates the monkey anatomically more than he does the true Caucasian; and when little or none of the face is anterior to the line, he approximates that mythical being of Dr. Van Evrie, a *black white man*, and almost ceases to be a negro. The black man occasionally seen in Africa, called the *Bature Dudu*, with high nose, thin lips, and long straight hair, is not a negro at all, but a Moor tanned by the climate—because his children, not exposed to the sun, do not become black like himself. The typical negro's nervous system is modelled a little different from the Caucasian and somewhat like the ourang outang. The medullary spinal cord is larger and more developed than in the white man, but less so than in the monkey tribes. The occipital foramen, giving exit to the spinal cord, is a third longer, says Cuvier, in proportion to its breadth, than in the Caucasian, and is so oblique as to form an angle of 30° with the horizon, yet not so oblique as in the simiadiæ, but sufficiently so to throw the head somewhat backwards and the face upwards in the erect position. Hence, from the obliquity of the head and the pelvis, the negro walks steadier with a weight on his head, as a pail of water for instance, than without it; whereas, the white man, with a weight on his head, has great difficulty in maintaining his centre of gravity, owing to the occipital foramen forming no angle with the cranium, the pelvis, the spine, or the thighs—all forming a straight line from the crown of the head to the sole of the foot without any of the obliquities seen in the negro's knees, thighs, pelvis and head—and still more evident in the ourang outang.

The nerves of organic life are larger in the prognathous species of mankind than in the Caucasian species, but not so well developed as in the simiadiæ. The brain is about a tenth smaller in the prognathous man than in the Frenchman, as proved by actual measurement of skulls by the French savans, Palisot and Virey. Hence, from the small brain and the larger nerves, the digestion of the prognathous species is better than that of the Caucasian and its animal appetites stronger, approaching the simiadæ but stopping short of their beastiality. The nostrils of the prognathous species of mankind open higher up than they do in the white or olive species, but not so high up as in the monkey tribes. In the gibbon, for instance, they open between the orbits. Although the typical negro's nostrils open high up, yet owing to the nasal bones being short and flat, there is no projection or prominence formed between his orbits by the bones of the nose, as in the Caucasian species. The nostrils, however, are much wider, about as wide from wing to wing, as the white man's mouth from corner to corner, and the internal bones, called the turbinated, on which the olfactory nerves are spread, are larger and project nearer to the opening of the nostrils than in the white man. Hence the negro approximates the lower animals in his sense of smell, and can detect snakes by that sense alone. All the senses are more acute, but less delicate and discriminating, than the white man's. He has a good ear for melody but not for harmony, a keen taste and relish for food but less discriminating between the different kinds of esculent substances than the Caucasian. His lips are immensely thicker than any of the white race, his nose broader and flatter, his chin smaller and more retreating, his foot flatter, broader, larger, and the heel longer, while he has scarcely any calves at all to his legs when compared to an equally healthy and muscular white man. He does not walk flat on his feet but on the outer sides, in consequence of the sole of the foot having a direction inwards, from the legs and thighs being arched outwards and the knees bent. The verb, from which his Hebrew name is derived, points out this flexed position of the knees, and also clearly expresses the servile type of his mind. Ham, the father of Canaan, when translated into plain English, reads that a black man was the father of the slave or knee-bending species of mankind.

The blackness of the prognathous race, known in the world's history as Canaanites, Cushites, Ethiopians, black men or negroes, is not confined to the skin, but pervades, in a greater or less degree, the whole inward man down to the bones themselves, giving the flesh and the blood, the membranes and every organ and part of the body, except the bones, a darker hue than in the white race. Who knows but what Canaan's mother may have been a genuine Cushite, as black inside as out, and that Cush, which means blackness, was the mark put upon Cain? Whatever may have been the mark set upon Cain, the negro, in all ages of the world, has carried with him a mark equally efficient in preventing him from being slain—the mark of blackness. The wild Arabs and hostile American Indians invariably catch the black wanderer and make a slave of him instead of killing him, as they do the white man.

Nich. Pechlin, in a work written last century entitled " De cute Athiopum," Albinus, in another work, entitled " De sede et causa coloris Athiop," as also the great German anatomists, Meiners, Ebel, and Sœmmering, all bear witness to the fact that the muscles, blood, membranes, and all the internal organs of the body, (the bones alone excepted,) are of a darker hue in the negro than in the white man. They estimate the difference in color to be equal to that which exists between the hare and the rabbit. Who ever doubts the fact, or has none of those old and impartial authorities at hand—impartial because they were written before England adopted the policy of pressing religion and science in her service to place white American republican freemen and Guinea negroes upon the same platform—has only to look into the mouth of the first healthy typical negro he meets to be convinced of the truth, that the entire membraneous lining of the inside of the cheeks, lips and gums is of a much darker color than in the white man.

The negro, however, must be healthy and in good condition—sickness, hard usage and chronic ailments, particularly that cachescia, improperly called consumption, speedily extracts the coloring matter out of the mucous membranes, leaving them paler and whiter than in the Caucasian. The bleaching process of bad health or degeneration begins in the blood, membranes and muscles, and finally extracts so much of the coloring pigment out of the skin, as to give it a dull, ashy appearance, sometimes extracting the whole of it, converting the negro into the albino. Albinoism or cucoris does not necessarily imply hybridism. It occurs among the pure Africans from any cause producing a degeneration of the species. Hybridism, however, is the most prolific source of that degeneration. Sometimes the degeneration shows itself by white spots, like the petals of flowers, covering different parts of the skin. The Mexicans are subject to a similar degeneration, only that the spots and stripes are black instead of white. It is called the pinto with them. Even the pigment of the iris and the coloring matter of the Albino's hair absorbed, giving it a silvery white appearance, and converting him into a clairvoyant at night. According to Professors Brown, Seidy and Gibbs, the negro's hair is not tubular, like the white man's, but it is excentrically elliptical with flattened edges, the coloring matter residing in the epidermis and not in tubes. In the place of a tube, the shaft of each hair is surrounded with a scaly covering like sheep's wool, and, like wool, is capable of being felted. True hair does not possess that property. The degeneration called Albinoism has a remarkable influence upon the hair, destroying its coarse, nappy, wooly appearance, and converting it into fine, long, soft, silky, curly threads. Often, the whole external skin, so remarkably void of hair in the healthy negro, becomes covered with a very fine, silky down, scarcely perceptible to the naked eye, when transformed into the Albino.

Mr. Bowen, the celebrated Baptist missionary, (see his work entitled Central Africa and Missionary Labors from 1849 to 1856, by T. J. Bowen, Charleston, Southern Baptist Publication Society, 1857,) met with a great many cases of leucosis in Soudan or Negroland back of Liberia, and erroneously concluded that these people had very little, if any negro blood in them, and would be better subjects for missionary labors than the blacks of the same country. They are, however, nothing but white black men, a degeneration of the negro proper, and are even less capable of perpetuating themselves than the hybrids or mulattoes. Mr. Bowen is at a loss to account for the depopulation, which he verifies has been going on in Soudan the last fifty years, threatening to leave the country, at no distant time, bare of inhabitants, unless roads be constructed by the Christians of the southern States for commercial intercourse, and double exertions made to civilise and Christianise the waning population of Central Africa before it entirely disappears. The good missionary, though sent out from Georgia, was evidently taught in that British school which assumes that there is only a single species in the genus homo, in opposition to the Bible, that clearly designates three. That school quotes the references in the sacred volume, implying unity in the genus—a unity which no one denies—to disprove the existence of distinct species, and upon this fallacy builds the theory that negro, Indian and white men are beings exactly alike, because they are human beings. *Ergo,* the liberty so beneficial to the white man, would be equally so to the negro—disregarding as a fable those words of the Bible expressly declaring that the latter *shall be servant of servants* to the former—words which would not have been there if that kind of subordination called slavery was not the normal condition of the race of Ham. To expect to civilise or Christianise the negro without the intervention of slavery is to expect an impossibility.

Mr. Bowen's experience and natural good sense occasionally got the better of his theoretical views. Thus, at page 90, we find him confessing that " the native African negroes ought to have masters in obedience to the demands of natural justice." At page 149 he lets us into the secret of the depopulating process which has been going on in Central Africa the last fifty years. While standing among some negroes in Ikata, a town in Central Africa, a capricious mulatto chief sent some officers among the company, who singled out a poor fellow who had offended the chief by saying that as he let a white man into town, he might let in a Dahomey man also, and presented him with an empty bag with the message, " The king says you must send me your head." The Rev. missionary, who was present at the beheading, made no comment further than to state the fact. But he might have added that the blood of that negro, and millions of others, will be required at the hands of Victoria Regina and the United States for having officiously destroyed the value of negro property in Africa by breaking up the only trade that ever protected the native Africans against the butcheries, cruelties and oppressions of their mulatto, Moorish and Mahommedan tyrants It is these butcheries and cruelties, and the little care taken of the black man in Africa, the last fifty years, since he became valueless through British and American philanthropy, that lie at the root of the depopulating process which is going on in the dark land of the Niger. Empty bags are now filled with heads instead of cowries. Mr. Bowen was surprised to see so few black men in Soudan, where, half a century ago, he says they were so numerous. But he rather regards it as a fortunate circumstance, as he has no hope of christianising the typical negro, except through slavery to Christian masters—and that idea is abhorrent to the school in which he was taught; but he has more hope from the mixed races, and these, he confesses, cannot be effectually christianised until civilised. He deplores the bad example of the black race, among them, their polygamy, &c., as greatly in the way of civilising the mulattoes. But he has overlooked the important fact, as many do, that the existence of the hybrids themselves depends upon the existence of the typical Africans. The extinction of the latter must, of necessity, be soon followed by the extinction of the former, as they cannot, for any length of time, propagate among themselves.

Mr. Bowen inferred that the negroes of Central Africa, although diminishing in numbers, are rising higher in the scale of humanity, from the very small circumstance that they do not emit from their bodies so strong and so offensive an odor as the negro slaves of Georgia and the Carolinas do, nor are their skins of so deep a black. This is a good illustration of the important truth, that all the danger of the slavery question lies in the ignorance of Scripture and the natural history of the negro. A little acquaintance with the negro's natural history would prove to Mr. Bowen that the strong odor emitted by the negro, like the deep pigment of the skin, is an indication of high health, happiness, and good treatment, while its deficiency is a sure sign of unhappiness, disease, bad treatment, or degeneration. The skin of a happy, healthy negro is not only blacker and more oily than an unhappy, unhealthy one, but emits the strongest odor when the body is warmed by exercise and the soul is filled with the most pleasurable emotions. In the dance called *patting juber*, the odor emitted from the men, intoxicated with pleasure, is often so powerful as to throw the negro women into paroxysms of unconsciousness, vulgo hysterics. On another point of much importance there is no practical difference between the Rev. missionary and that clear-headed, bold, and eccentric old Methodist, Dr. McFarlane. Both believe that the Bible can do ignorant, sensual savages no good; both believe that nothing but compulsory power can restrain uncivilised barbarians from polygamy, inebriety, and other sinful practices.

The good missionary, however, believes in the possibility of civilising the inferior races by the money and means of the Christian nations lavishly bestowed, after which he thinks it will be no difficult matter to convert them to Christianity. Whereas the venerable Methodist believes in the impossibility of civilising them, and therefore concludes that the Written Word was not intended for those inferior races who cannot read it. When the philosophy of the prognathous species of mankind is better understood, it will be seen how they, the lowest of the human species, can be made partakers, equally with the highest, in the blessings and benefits of the Written Word of God. The plantation laws against polygamy, intoxicating drinks and other besetting sins of the negro race in the savage state, are gradually and silently converting the African barbarian into a moral, rational and civilised being, thereby rendering the heart a fit tabernacle for the reception of Gospel truths. The prejudices of many, perhaps the majority of the southern people, against educating the negroes they hold in subjection, arise from some vague and indefinite fears of its consequences, suggested by the Abolition and British theories built on the false assumption that the negro is a white man with a black skin. If such an assumption had the smallest degree of truth in it, the more profound the ignorance and the deeper sunk in barbarism the slaves were kept, the better it would be for them and their masters. But experience proves that masters and overseers have nothing at all to fear from civilised and intelligent negroes and no trouble whatever in managing them—that all the trouble, insubordination and danger arise from the uncivilised, immoral, rude, and grossly ignorant portion of the servile race. It is not the ignorant semi-barbarian that the master or overseer entrusts with his keys, his money, his horse or his gun, but the most intelligent on the plantation—one whose intellect and morals have undergone the best training. An educated negro, one whose intellect and morals have been cultivated, is worth double the price of the wild, uncultivated, black barbarian of Cuba, and will do twice as much work, do it better and with less trouble.

The prejudices against educating the negroes may also be traced to the neglect of American divines in making themselves acquainted with Hebrew literature. What little the most of them know of the meaning of the untranslated terms occuring in the Bible, and the signification of the verbs from which they are derived, is mostly gathered from British commentators and glossary makers, who have blinked the facts that disprove the Exeter Hall dogma, that negro slavery is sin against God. Hence, even in the South, the important biblical truth, that the white man derives his authority to govern the negro from the Great Jehovah, is seldom proclaimed from the pulpit. If it were proclaimed, the master race would see deeper into their responsibilities and look closer into the duties they owe to the people whom God has given them as an inheritance, and their children after them, so long as time shall last. That man has no faith in the Scriptures who believes that education could defeat God's purposes, in subjecting the black man to the government of the white. On the contrary, experience proves its advantages, to both parties. Aside and apart from Scripture authority, natural history reveals most of the same facts, in regard to the negro that the Bible does. It proves the existence of at least three distinct species of the genus man, differing in their instincts, form, habits and color. The white species having qualities denied to the black—one with a free and the other with a servile mind—one a thinking and reflective being, the other a creature of feeling and imitation, almost void of reflective faculties, and consequently unable to provide for and take care of himself. The relation of master and slave would naturally spring up between two such different species of men, even if there was no Scripture authority to support it. The relation thus established, being natural, would be drawn closer together, instead of severed, by the inferior imitating the superior in all his ways, or in other words, acquiring an education.